Danger on
Shadow Mountain

Weekly Reader Children's Book Club
presents

Danger on Shadow Mountain

MARIAN RUMSEY

illustrated by
LYDIA ROSIER

William Morrow and Company
New York

For my niece, Sharon

By the Same Author

Beaver of Weeping Water
Devil's Doorstep
High Country Adventure
The Seal of Frog Island
Shipwreck Bay

Table of Contents

1 Trouble on Pine Island   9

2 The Lure of Shadow Mountain   17

3 Digging Out   26

4 Alone   35

5 Killers on the Sound   44

6 Indian Camp   57

7 Jackstraw   64

8 Swamped   75

9 A Narrow Escape   84

10 Marooned   93

11 Over the River   100

12 Base Camp   111

13 The Climb   120

14 Over the Top   131

15 Scratch One Helicopter   139

16 Two Bagged Birds   149

Danger on
Shadow Mountain

CHAPTER 1

Trouble on Pine Island

It was nearly noon, but the thick mist still hid the island in a grayish shroud. Pete Fleming had been standing under a pine tree, hoping for sound of the boat. He was wet and uncomfortable, and to make matters even worse, the faintest waft of a breeze had come up from the north. The old tree must have swayed ever so slightly, for a steady drip of dew fell from its heights and crackled the soggy mat of undercover.

Pete was dreadfully impatient to see his brother, and this waiting certainly was not helping at all. He had been on Pine Island only a few days, and most of the time he had been working on Dave's new launch, giving it a good shiny polish so that it gleamed like gold. Earlier, that very morning, his brother had gone down the coast to deliver supplies, and he had promised to take Pete across the island to go fishing when he returned. Pete stared gloomily at the fog. If it kept up, Dave probably would be delayed, and they would have to postpone their outing for yet another day.

Pete turned up his collar and, with his back to the wind, began to think of the gooseberry pie that he and Dave had made after breakfast waiting to be eaten. He slapped his hands under his armpits like a flailing bird to warm himself, then watched water drip from the tip of his hat brim until his eyes crossed. At last he grinned to himself. No matter how miserable he was at that moment, he thought staying on Pine Island for always would be the neatest thing ever. His brother was the luckiest person in the world to live on the Pacific Coast of British Columbia and in a place so remote it could be reached only by boat.

Last year had been Pete's first visit. It had been great fun. Dave wasn't fussy about things like neatness or being sparkling clean all the time. And, someday, Pete hoped he could persuade his brother to add his name to the Dave Fleming Island Service. For over a hundred miles of territory, Dave supplied and delivered the necessities of living to the lonely inhabitants of islands and coves on the inside passage to Alaska.

Never would he be lonely on Pine Island. Why, last year during his stay there he had helped work the trotline and the crab pots. Dave had taught him how to trap and how to tan a hide. And there were special days, like the one they had watched a seemingly endless string of geese pass overhead as they winged south.

So much was going to happen this year; he knew his summer would have a wonderful end.

Swirls of mists weaved through the limbs of the pine tree like cotton gauze, making the visibility very poor. There was the slightest rustle of pine needles, the distant, lonesome call of a bird, and off to the right the babble of water as the tide rushed around the bend. Hearing a faint sound, Pete bent his head and stared at the tips of his boots, tense and listening hard. When he looked up, he knew Dave had come at last.

Quickly Pete ran down the edge of trees, leaped the small bank that separated him from the rocky beach, then went along the shore until he came to the first oil drum filled with driftwood. He jerked off the lid, ripped off his gloves, and pawed through his pocket for the box of matches. A small tin of coal oil was sitting inside the drum, and he splashed it over the brush and tossed the can aside. His hands were cold, and he was working as if in slow motion. He pushed the lighted match into the scraps of fuzz Dave had saved from some old caulking cotton and watched the first burst of smoke. Suddenly the flame caught the oil, and the drum flared with a gigantic *wroomp!*

Pete stepped back and gawked at it stupidly, startled half out of his wits as the flame shot up. He turned to the next barrel and lit it with the same results.

Stumbling over a half-rusted wagon rim, Pete tripped and nearly fell, just as the boat loomed out of the haze. Already it was slowing down, coming in for a bumpy, uneven landing. He bounded across the dock and waved his arms like a welcoming loony bird. Dave cut the engine and at the same moment tossed the bow line over a bollard and handed Pete the stern line.

"Hi, there, boy!" Dave said to him with a thump on the back. "Must say I appreciate those Pine Island lighthouses." He pointed to the lighted barrels. "Fog's thick as soup up here." Pete grinned as his brother grabbed him around the neck and gave him a playful shake, just as a brownish blot leaped out of the boat.

"Crackers!" Pete gasped. Dave's familiar little dog barked and ran to him. "You crazy coyote," Pete said, as he snatched her by the tail and let himself be whirled in dizzy circles. Then she let out another howl, shook Pete loose, and ran straight for the woods.

"Am I ever glad you're back," said Pete.

Dave chuckled. "Now don't tell me you were scared being here all alone for a few hours."

Pete glared at him. "No. But you did promise to go fishing, remember?"

"Have you dug the worms?"

Pete grinned and nodded, delighted they would be off at last for the rest of the day on their own.

"Then help me unload," Dave said, and handed him a canvas bag of gear. "I've got the mail and—"

Unexpectedly a sound came from overhead. It was so startling they stopped in their tracks and stared into the sky. The noise quickly became much louder, coming in great, swooshing thumps.

"A helicopter!" exclaimed Dave incredulously, and he dropped the coil of heavy line he had taken from the launch.

Pete strained to see the plane while Dave hurriedly jumped to the beach, nearly trampling Crackers as she ran out of the brush alarmed by the sudden noise. "He—he's awfully close," Pete said anxiously. Hearing such a paralyzing noise so near at hand, and yet not being able to see where it came from, was unnerving.

"He must have sighted those lighted barrels," Dave shouted. "I only hope he can see better up there than—" Suddenly the trees bent to a sudden blast of wind, and the sound of the engine became nearly deafening.

Pete gasped, and Crackers cowered beneath him, terrified. The helicopter, looking as evil as some great, gray hawk, abruptly burst into sight and came straight for them.

It frightened Pete so dreadfully he dove for what protection the rocks on the beach might give and sprawled face down in the stones. When he glanced up a second later, he saw Dave half crouched on the bank, waving his billed hat furiously. Then the plane began to wobble upward, and it swooped over their cabin with what seemed only inches to spare.

Pete staggered to his knees just as the earsplitting roar faded into silence. "Did they crash?" he choked, but Dave did not hear him, since he already was run-

ning down the path. By the time Pete untangled himself from Crackers, his brother was out of sight in the
mists. "Wait!" he croaked, but Crackers ran in and
out through his legs, tripping him. "Watch out--" he
gasped, and shoved the dog aside, only to stumble and
fall to his knees again.

When he finally reached the meadow, he was much
relieved to see the plane had landed and was all in one
piece. Although the rotors were still spinning, the two
men already had jumped out the cabin door. As Pete
panted up to them, he could tell immediately that his
brother was angry.

"Say, you nearly sat that thing down right on my
roof," Dave growled.

"Sorry about that," said one of the men, a heavy,
rough-looking sort with a worn jacket that had a patch
on one elbow. The other was shorter, with a pinched
face and shifty eyes. He tugged a duffle bag and a
large leather camera case out the door of the plane behind him, shrugged them over his shoulder, then turned
and brought out a shotgun, which he slung over his
arm.

"Where are you from?" Dave asked. "Bella Bella?"

"You Dave Fleming?" was the brusque answer.

Dave nodded cautiously, and a little reluctantly.
"I'm afraid you have the wrong place. I run the supply
boat out of Pine Island. This isn't a hunting camp."

"We know that," mumbled the big man. "You got a
place to put us up till this soup lifts?"

Dave chewed at his lip. Pete knew his brother wasn't at all happy with the two men, although he nodded. "Yes, certainly. You can't take off in this fog."

"Where's your cabin?" demanded the short, sharp-featured stranger who held the gun.

Dave motioned down the path, again a little reluctantly, then shrugged and started out. The men fell into line behind him. Pete took a last glance at the helicopter just as the rotor whistled to a final stop and followed, bringing up the rear.

It was an unwritten law of the North that, come bad weather, anyone seeking shelter was welcome in one's home. Last year, many times, fishermen had stopped for the night at Dave's dock to wait out fog or stormy weather, and those times Pete remembered as the very high spots of his visit. For Dave seemed to know nearly everyone, and these occasions always meant a dinner with a friend and a wonderful evening of talk around a roaring fire. Then when the weather improved, they always said good-bye reluctantly to the stranded visitor, as he started off in fair weather. Yet from the beginning the two men from the helicopter were different.

CHAPTER 2

The Lure of Shadow Mountain

Pete had spent part of the morning tidying the cabin when Dave was away on his supply run, and for once things were neatly put away and orderly. The fire he had built up earlier still sparked a bit of flame, and the kettle on the stove now and then hissed a puff of steam. The pie was sitting on the checkered tablecloth, the coffeepot was ready to be put on to perk. Although the cabin they all came into looked friendly, the strangers didn't notice. They shuffled inside, shoved the bags and the gun on the table, and when Dave motioned them to the two easy chairs, they flopped down in them, only to stare back at him warily. At last the man with the patched jacket spoke up, with the barest trace of effort to be pleasant. "We came up here special, just to talk to you."

Dave put the coffeepot on the stove and raised his eyebrows. "Oh?"

Pete threw a log on the fire, then sat quietly beside it, out of the way.

"My name's Jasper Hugo. This here is Benny Lud-low."

Dave pulled a straight-backed chair to the table, faced them, and sat down. "How'ja do," he said agreeably. Then with a slight nod. "My brother."

The men's eyes shifted to Pete, and as they stared at him moodily, he felt a faint sense of uneasiness.

"We thought you worked the supply boat alone," said the man called Jasper.

Dave nodded. "I do, most of the time. Pete just came up to spend a month with me before school starts."

Their eyes shifted back to Dave, and Pete relaxed slightly.

"What was it you wanted to see me about?" Dave asked sociably. When the strangers did not answer at once, he went on, "I really don't take out parties to hunt, you know. I just haven't the time. But if that's why you came up, I'll be glad to send you over to one of the best guides in the province."

"It's not that at all," said the man named Benny. "We want you to take us up to Shadow Mountain."

"Shadow Mountain!" exclaimed Dave, stunned. He stared at them in amazement. "Why on earth do you want to go there? Is it the mine? Do you want to go up to the old Shadow Mountain Mine?"

A measured look passed between the two strangers,

and again Pete felt that touch of foreboding. He wiped his tongue over his lips nervously.

"You know about the mine then?" Jasper asked.

"Of course, I know about it," said Dave sharply. "Everyone around here knows about it. After all, it's not any secret."

"Then you could find your way up there?"

Dave shrugged noncommittally. "The Indians destroyed the trail years ago, and they don't cotton much to outsiders going up the mountain."

"But you been there?" Jasper insisted irritably. "We heard tell you been there."

Dave frowned at him. "Yes. Once. But it was a long time ago."

"All you need do is show us the mine," Jasper continued. "We'll get you up there in the chopper."

Dave shook his head. "Those digs are abandoned. Don't you know they were worked out twenty years ago? Besides, there never was much silver anyway. The place is so totally inaccessible it never paid even the Indians to mine it."

"Look," Benny complained shrilly. "All you got to do is take us there, not dig."

Dave sighed. "But you don't understand at all. That mine is only a memory, and, like I said, nowadays the Indians just don't want outsiders on the mountain."

"They don't own it!" snarled Benny.

Dave nodded. "That's true. What lease they had with the government expired years ago. But the mine is in an ancient tribal burial ground. It's sacred land to them."

"We'll offer you five hundred dollars," tempted Jasper.

"Look," Dave protested angrily, "can't you see that I just don't want to take you there? The Indians are my friends, and if they don't want strangers on Shadow Mountain I certainly would never take you, no matter how much money you offered me."

"Then that's it," Benny hissed, and with a practiced motion he had the shotgun in his hands and pointed straight at Dave's chest before either Pete or Dave realized it. "Now you'll take us!" he snarled. "Only with this in your back!"

Dave leaped out of his chair. At the same instant, with one quick pump of his arm, Benny levered a shell into the chamber ready to fire.

"Watch out!" Pete shouted.

He didn't think his brother would have stopped despite the gun, but Crackers brought him up short. The dog bounded across the room and leaped happily against his leg. Slightly off balance, Dave gave Jasper just enough time to pull a revolver from his jacket. With one quick step the man had Pete by the shoulder and the barrel of the gun pressed hard against his head.

Dave stopped in mid-stride. "Let the boy go," he flared.

Pete could feel the sweat standing out on his forehead. Jasper's grip was like iron, the barrel of the gun cold against his skin. He felt weak and sick, and he was desperately afraid.

"Sit down in that chair," Jasper ordered Dave, his voice quiet and very deadly.

Dave glared at him furiously, then, carefully, helplessly, did as he was told. "You'll never get away with this," he said bitterly.

Jasper shrugged, shoved Pete roughly against the wall, and pushed the gun against his neck. Pete licked his lips and watched his brother with wild, frantic eyes.

Immediately Jasper ordered his partner, "Start collecting supplies we can use. Food is the most important." He turned to Dave. "You got a cold cellar? Most of these outback cabins got one loaded for winter."

"Under the rug," Dave said between his teeth.

Benny moved quickly and pushed aside the oval braided rug in the center of the room. Beneath it was a trapdoor, with a round pick-up hole in the center. When he jerked it up, Pete could see the dark, unpleasant cavern below. There was a ladder propped against one side, and Benny swung onto it and disappeared into the darkness.

Jasper shoved Pete into motion and to the desk beside the window. With a wary eye on Dave he shuffled the papers on the desk top with the barrel of the gun. In a moment he found Dave's supply schedule and glanced through it quickly. Then with a sly grin he turned to Dave. "So this was the last run for the week, eh?"

Pete felt his spirits sink dreadfully. He knew that Dave was not due to make another run for over seven days. No one along the sound would be expecting his brother, so no one would worry when he did not arrive, a perfect arrangement for the two men.

At that moment Benny heaved a khaki canvas bag out from the cellar. Pete saw it was filled with a few of Dave's stored home supplies. There was a ham, a batch of runty potatoes still coated with dirt, some puny cabbages, and a few wilted carrots. Benny climbed back up and slammed the door with a crash. "That's all that's down there worth bothering about," he whined with a sulky look at Dave. Then he began to empty cupboards, adding a bit more to his meager cache. Next he rolled up the blankets on both beds and finally tossed a pick and shovel stored beside the door with the rest. "Nothin' else," he said shortly.

Jasper pulled Pete to the fireplace, picked up the ax, and then turned unexpectedly to the radio cabinet beside the desk. He swung the heavy weapon with all his strength, and the force of the blow shattered the instrument into a mangled mass of metal and wire. Pete began shaking uncontrollably. The radio transmitter had been their one hope. Through it they somehow might have been able to get help from the police in Bella Bella.

"Now to get rid of the boat," Jasper told his partner, while Dave seethed in angry frustration.

"Do what?" Dave exclaimed sharply.

"I'll see to it," Benny said knowingly, and took the ax from Jasper.

"There may be more than one," Jasper told him. "So be sure you check thoroughly."

"What are you going to do?" Dave demanded, half rising from his chair.

"Sit down," Jasper snapped, and gave Dave a menacing glance, only to have Crackers suddenly leap around him with the enthusiasm of an overgrown puppy. "Get that mutt out of here," he snarled to Benny with a vicious kick at the dog, but, as usual, Crackers danced about with all the elusiveness of a slippery snake.

Before long, perhaps ten minutes, Benny returned. "Well?" Jasper demanded impatiently.

"There was this one big boat and two little skiffs."

"You took care of them?"

Benny smiled. "All that's left is kindling."

Jasper then turned to Dave, and said, "You get us up to Shadow Mountain and to the mine. That's all we want of you. Do it, and I'll see that this kid here comes out all right."

Pete looked at Dave with an appalling wave of fear.

"What do you mean by that?" Dave demanded.

For an answer Benny pulled up the trapdoor once again, and Jasper turned to Pete. "Get down there, sonny."

Pete gasped, startled, and stepped back.

"Come on, come on. We haven't got all night." The

man took him harshly by the shoulder and started to pull him toward the dark pit.

"No!" Pete wailed. He had hardly spoken when Dave was on his feet. Benny must have been expecting him, because he brought the butt of the shotgun down on Dave's head with a crash.

Afterward everything happened quickly. Pete gaped in horror as Dave slumped forward across the table, not quite unconscious, but nearly out on his feet. The next moment Jasper took Pete around the neck and lowered him kicking and squirming down into the dark.

By the time the man turned him loose and he felt the firmness of a floor under him, Crackers squealed and came flying down, landing on his shoulders. They both fell and rolled out flat. Then the trapdoor crashed shut with a loud thud, and before Pete could untangle himself from the dog, he heard some heavy object being dragged over the door to keep it securely closed.

"Keep still," he said frantically to Crackers. She was jumping around so much Pete couldn't hear what was being said in the room above them. "I said keep still!" he ordered again, then reached out and took the dog by her harness and held her quiet against his jacket.

"Get this stuff down to the plane." Jasper was talking, his voice muffled and distant. "Get a move on you."

"What's the big idea putting the boy down there?" said Dave. His voice was gruff and a little unsteady. He must not have been badly hurt from the clout on his head.

"He can stay there till doomsday," mumbled Benny. "Unless you do as you're told. Come on, let's go. It will take a half hour to load."

"You're crazy as coots," raged Dave darkly.

"Pipe down, you! And pick up that gear! Benny, grab that bag, and let's go."

"You can't leave that boy in there," Dave shouted again.

"We can and we will," said Jasper unpleasantly. "But if you do as we tell you, we'll bring you back to this island and release the kid."

"But he's only twelve. He can't manage alone."

"Quiet!" Jasper snarled. "Or do you want Benny to knock you down again?"

Dave must have moved, for when he spoke he was standing right over Pete, his voice loud and very clear. "You've taken most of the food. How do you think he's going to survive?"

Jasper apparently was ignoring him again as he collected their belongings. Benny spoke then. "We can use that coil of rope hanging on the rafters. And that pair of binoculars."

"Crikey!" fumed Dave finally. "You're both daft!"

There was a great deal of movement then, footsteps, and the sliding and adjusting of gear. The voices suddenly grew fainter and became only a muffled jumble until, at last, they were gone altogether. And in the bottom of the cold cellar there was nothing but darkness and silence.

CHAPTER 3

Digging Out

Crackers whined suddenly, squirmed and wiggled, and Pete put her down to the floor. He couldn't see her in the blackness, but he touched her long ears. He was dreadfully frightened just then and got a brief comfort from the cheerful lick she gave his hand.

Pete's first panicky thought was to try to get out the trapdoor. The hatch didn't really fit well, and the faintest glimmer of light from the room was filtering down to him from around one edge.

Climbing the ladder wasn't at all easy. It was a single pole with steps lashed haphazardly across the center. They were rickety, and his feet kept sliding off the ends in his rush. When he got up a few feet, his head immediately banged on the ceiling of the cellar with a crash. Crackers whined and jumped about beneath him.

Pete rubbed his head, then pushed at the door. It didn't move. Using both hands was difficult because of his precarious balance, so he tried to shove it with his shoulder. Whatever the men had dragged over the door on top was far heavier than he could lift at such an angle and with so poor a foothold.

Pete rested momentarily on the step of the ladder. There was not the slightest sound above him. By now they all must be far along the path. Quickly he pulled out his sheath knife and tried to chisel at the underside of the door, but the wood was like iron.

If only the cellar wasn't so dark! It was awful! Pete wished frantically he had a flashlight. But why would he be carrying around a flashlight in the middle of the day? Then he stopped, sucked in his breath, and scrambled down to the floor.

Crackers immediately jumped wildly around his feet, making him lose his balance, and he fell to his knees. Quickly he shuffled through his pockets and found the box of matches he had used to light the fuel drums earlier in the day.

"I've got them," he said in a choked voice. Crackers barked shrilly and drenched his face with her tongue. Moreover, he had a whole box. Pete scratched one match, and then scratched again, and when the flame came it was a most welcome sight.

"Wow!" he exclaimed with a start, and grabbed shakily at a candle that was sitting on a box right beside him. When the wick caught, he blew out the match and stood for a moment holding it smoking in his hand. He was in a cave, a dark and gloomy place that was cold and very damp. There was another pack of matches on the box, which Dave must have left to light the candle.

Pete walked slowly around the small cellar. He had been in the place only once, and that was last year. It hadn't appealed to him very much, and so he always had let Dave come down for what few supplies they had needed. Now he could see the cellar was lined with roughly built shelves, filled to brimming with bottles and jars. There were a few cans of food, too, and baskets of vegetables on the floor edging the racks. And there were spiders; he wiped the sticky webs from his face. He needed only a minute to see there was no way out but overhead.

The candle was set in a tin-can holder, and Pete swung it down to the earthen floor, looking for something with which to chop, hopefully an ax. He searched again, unhappy about the black bugs that darted out from under baskets he chanced to disturb. But there was nothing.

At last he came back and stood beneath the hatch another time. The ceiling was quite high and deep in gloom. He possibly might be able to tear down a shelf and use it to poke at the trapdoor and force it up. The largest of the boards might just be long enough to reach that far. He brushed at the spider webs again; they were everywhere and felt horrible.

Quickly he began to unload one shelf. He wondered what was in all the bottles Dave had stored there, and finally he unscrewed the cap of one and sniffed.

Crackers came up to smell, too.

"It's beer!" He put it down and went back to work. At least he wouldn't die of thirst, he thought half hysterically. But then he didn't like beer. He had drunk about four swallows one time at his uncle's birthday party and had thought it was pretty grim stuff.

He shoved the last of the bottles to the ground with a rattle of glass and yanked at the wood. Luckily, it wasn't nailed down, and with a certain amount of adjusting he worked it out of its place. It was barely long enough to reach the ceiling above him. He took hold of one end and pounded violently against the trapdoor. Then he put his full weight to it and pushed as hard as he could, but without the slightest success.

Pete dropped the plank and climbed quickly back up the ladder. His hands were shaking now, and he was getting more terrified by the second. He carried the light this time and shined it on the underside of the door. Perhaps he could do something to the hinges.

Suddenly he gasped. There was a piece of paper pushed through the crack, one he hadn't seen in the darkness! He snatched it, lost his balance, and came flying to the floor with a crash.

Crackers barked wildly as he unfolded the paper. It had been creased so often it looked like an accordion. He collected the candle from the dirt and shined it on the hastily scribbled writing. *Dig out ice hatch.*

Pete held the paper closer to the light. "Dig out ice hatch?" he said aloud. Obviously Dave had managed to slip him the note before they all left the cabin. But whatever did it mean?

Pete frowned. A hatch on a boat was a top that went over an opening. But he didn't know what an ice hatch was exactly. Once more he held the flame above his head and looked carefully over the ceiling. There simply wasn't another opening up there, only the one through which he had been dropped so unceremoniously.

Yet if his brother had left him the message, he surely must have known what he was talking about. There must be something in the place beside beer and jarred blackberries. He wished desperately he had visited the cellar with Dave more often last year. Once more, slowly and methodically, Pete began to work his way around the room. It was very quiet, the only sounds the soft pad of Crackers' feet as she followed him and the sputter of the candle as it drooled wax into a filmy puddle on the holder. Everything smelled damp; the mustiness of vegetables and dirt was heavy in the air.

Eventually he found what he was looking for. There was a hatch, after all, only it was on the side of a wall, half hidden in the dark behind some rotting fishing nets. It was about a yard square, held in place by two slabs of wood turned as a lock. Pete's fingers were shaky when he tried the fastening, but found it opened easily. The whole door came off in his hands, and an icy waft of air swept out to him. He leaned down eagerly to look inside.

"Oh!" He got a really bad turn then. When he shined the light closer, all he could see was blood. He clamped his hand unsteadily over his lips, but it was only meat Dave had stored away in ice and snow.

He scooped some of the white spattered stuff up in his hand and felt its cold wetness. There were some skinned rabbits or squirrels, and a leg of something, probably a deer. It all looked horrible, but he guessed Dave had to have an icebox. He still could not see any way out. The small space was packed solid with ice and snow.

"What-are-you-doing!" he said shortly to Crackers. She was busily digging beside him, kicking snow over his feet. Then she began to tug at the leg of meat and dragged it heavily across the dirt floor of the cellar, where she settled contentedly in a corner to feast.

Pete kneeled on the floor and began to scoop out the snow. If Dave said dig, that must be the thing to do. He would need to burrow upward to the place where all the ice had come from in the first place. There must be a door somewhere through the thick drift over his head, and he would have to find it. He shivered, his teeth chattering loudly in the quiet.

He dug steadily, shoving the snow back into the cellar. It started to melt in the warmth of the little room, and the earthen floor soon became muddy and unpleasant. Behind him he could hear Crackers smacking and grinding as she enjoyed her meal.

More and more snow collected as he pushed and

shoved it aside. He climbed inside the icebox and tunneled upward. Now and again he was forced to stop to warm his hands by shoving them inside his sweater against his warm chest. It was dig and shovel, dig and shovel, until finally he hit something solid.

He scraped furiously overhead, his heart pounding excitedly. Then he crept back to get the candle so that he could see properly what he had come up against. It was definitely wood.

"Oh, but I'm f-f-freezing," Pete moaned. He was surrounded on all sides by snow and ice, and the cold sent him into uncontrollable spasms of shivering.

It took all of a half hour, by which time he was thoroughly chilled to the very marrow, before he found the hasp and hinge of the door that led outside. He didn't know what he would do if it wouldn't open or if it was locked. But Dave would have known about that. He dug furiously and cleared the last ice to one side.

Crackers pawed up beside him, dragging her partially devoured bone. Pete shoved her roughly aside, and with both hands over his head he pushed with every ounce of his strength.

The door flew back so easily it slammed over and away from him with a crash. Pete scrambled up over the sill and stood shivering in the grass. He had come up behind the cabin, and he could not ever remember when the world looked quite so good.

Then he was off running around the house to the front porch. He burst in the door and skidded to a stop in the center of the room. The heavy oaken desk was over the trapdoor, and a rope tied between the fireplace and the window held it in place. No amount of pushing from below ever would have moved it.

"The plane!" he gasped frantically. He knew well enough it probably would be gone. Hours had passed since he had been tossed down the cellar.

He dashed out the door and fled down the path as fast as he could go. He wasn't at all keen on meeting Jasper and Benny with their guns, but he was far, far more frightened of being left alone on Pine Island.

CHAPTER 4
Alone

Pete came to a breathless halt on the edge of the meadow and stood knee-deep in the waving grass. "They're gone," he said shakily, as he stared at the great flattened path in mid-field and the footprints that led out to it. He turned slightly and gazed into the again thickening mist. Shadow Mountain was the highest peak around, yet he could see nothing of it now, only silent swirls of fog. There was a soft and eerie moan of wind in the pines, and somewhere, far off, came the hollow cry of a gull. Pete shivered. Suddenly he wanted to look at the launch. Perhaps it had not really been sunk after all.

He ran again, through grass and bracken and thorny blackberry brambles, jumping over fallen stumps. Then he scrambled over the bank and out to the rocky beach. The stones rolled underfoot and clattered into

35

the water like wet marbles as he stopped before the dock.

Benny had done a thorough job with the ax. The two rowboats were in bits and pieces and floated in the wavelets along the water's rocky edge. The worst disaster, however, was Dave's shining new launch. Pete bit his lip hopelessly. Only a section of the bow was showing above water, the torn, splintered wood evidence it never could be repaired.

Pete sank down on the rocks and looked at the cold, gray water. He couldn't recall when he ever had felt so frightened. He wanted now to be inside the cabin, to be warm, and out of the ghostly fog. Rocks and logs took on weird and unreal shapes. Stumps looked like headless monsters rising from the smoky depths of the earth itself. The dew that dripped from the trees sounded like sinister footsteps.

He ran his tongue over his lips quickly. For some reason he abruptly remembered Dave's old fishing skiff, one he long since had replaced with the two that now lay wrecked along the shore. Crackers barked and dragged her bone up to his feet. Pete touched her gently and rather absently. He had not seen the old dinghy this year, but he knew it once had been kept on the leeward side of the island up one of the small creeks.

Pete got to his feet. "Come on," he said to Crackers, not especially eager to go exploring in the last light by himself. With the dog he circled the small island

and reached the farthest shore before stopping to get his bearings. They went on another hundred feet, only to hesitate uncertainly. There was no sign of the rowboat. Perhaps Dave no longer had the skiff. Or worse yet, maybe those two men had cast it adrift.

"Crackers?" Now the little dog had disappeared, and Pete whistled shrilly. "Crackers!" He heard her bark not far away and quickly ran up a path leading inland. A few moments later he found her jumping frantically at the base of a pine while a bushy-tailed squirrel scurried overhead. He took the dog by her harness impatiently, then stopped dead in his tracks. There was the boat right in front of him! It was half hidden by brush and leaves.

The boat wasn't much, he could tell that right off, and it made him feel uneasy. The closest help was a long way off, and the little rowboat looked far from being a very suitable craft in which to get there. It was pulled up on the grass, and the tiny creek in which it had been floated inland was hardly more than a trickle. Pete walked around the skiff examining it carefully.

He found a hole in it, first thing. But it was up high and wouldn't be underwater unless the waves were awfully big. He kneeled on the grass and ran his hand over one side of the hull, then pulled the oars out from under the floorboards and looked at the inside of the hull. It surely wasn't very sturdy-looking. Dave must have tools somewhere, and he could nail a patch over the hole.

Gripping the gunwale tightly, Pete realized he must be planning on taking the skiff down the coast. What else could he do? He sat down on the rail of the boat wearily. Crackers jumped into his lap, and he hugged her tightly.

He had made the trip up Chikamin Sound with his brother only a few times, and he wished now he had paid more attention to distances. There had been stops —supplies he had helped load, mail they had delivered. Bella Bella was over forty miles away, he knew, on the coast at the entrance of the sound, which branched east off the inside passage to Alaska. The nearest settlement was at Indian Camp, where they had unloaded fishing gear. Again he turned to the south; there on clear days hulking Shadow Mountain loomed ominously across the water.

Pete thought of Indian Camp down the shore some ten or fifteen miles. If he did go, the worst part probably would be crossing Chikamin Sound, for Pine Island was nearly a mile away from the mainland. He would have to wait for the outgoing tide, too, since he never could row against the current when it was coming in. He shivered suddenly and looked through the trees in the direction of the beach. The tide would turn again about five in the morning.

Pete shoved Crackers away nervously. With a struggle he managed to tip the whole boat on its side, and then he examined it very thoroughly. It obviously had not been in the water for ages. Worms and bugs dis-

turbed by the move scuttled for shelter. One black bee-
tle darted across Crackers' foot, and she danced away
after it. Pete knew he must get the boat down to the
water and see if it would even float. He lowered it back
to the ground with a bump and studied the tiny creek.
Whenever Dave had pulled the boat into this shelter,
the stream must have been quite full or else the tide
much higher than it was at that moment. However,
Pete was sure if he once got it into the creek, it would
slide along over the mud to the open sound.

He pulled and tugged, struggling with it, for the
skiff was old and very heavy. The paint had peeled, the
wood had rotted in many places along the rail, and he
got splinters in his hands. Pete sank to his ankles in
the thick mud, and it splashed up into his face. Crackers
barked and jumped around on the drier ground, then
finally waded out to join him and splashed him even
more as he pushed the boat toward open water.

"This is awful," he mumbled to himself. He had
gone nearly the entire distance and gave one final shove.
Somehow the skiff slipped out of his grasp, skidded
through the slime, out of the creek, and into the main
sound. If he hadn't run and caught hold of the stern,
it would have sailed out beyond reach.

He was so tired he was nearly in tears. What if it had
gone out into the current and he had lost it? He set his
lips tightly and waded into the water. At least, he was
pleased to see there were no leaks in the bottom, and
the hole in the side was well above water line. He felt

sure he could put some sort of patch over it. Nevertheless, the skiff was not exactly his idea of a yacht even if it did float.

If only he was closer to town and the police. But the distance to Bella Bella might as well have been to China. Trying to find his way in the maze of islands to that village was out of the question.

It was getting very dark quickly, now that the fog once more had settled in thickly, and work on the boat would have to be done in the morning. It got light at four, so he would have an hour before the tide changed and he could start. He pulled the boat above high water mark and left it till then.

Peter settled in for the night in Dave's cabin. It was a comfortable home, its untidiness now due simply to the men's haste to get away in the helicopter. Chairs were tipped, the desk and table littered with papers. The braided rugs were messily stirred, and drawers in chests and cupboards were cocked half open, the contents spewing out in heaps.

There were four kerosene lamps, and Pete lit them all to make everything more cheerful. Having lived with Dave before, he at least knew how to build up the fire in the big wood stove. He rummaged through cupboards, found some tinned beef and beans, and after finally locating the can opener stuffed beneath the silverware, he began to fix a meal. Next he rebuilt the fire in the stone fireplace, and though it smoked some when he first started it, soon it was crackling pleasantly.

Now he felt more like facing the night ahead. By that time his meat and beans were heated, and he brought them to the easy chair to eat before the fire. Crackers was roasting on the rug before him, her back hot to the touch.

Afterward, as he washed up the dishes, he wondered if perhaps he was being a little foolish about trying to row across the sound to Indian Camp. He could live very pleasantly in Dave's cabin. Eventually someone would become concerned when his brother failed to return to Bella Bella and would start a search for Dave and the launch. They would find him, and he could give them word of what had happened.

Pete went back to the fire and curled up in the chair. The logs were burning low, and Crackers twitched in puppy dreams, her bone safely tucked under her paw. But what would happen to his brother if he failed to go for help now? What would Jasper and Benny do to him once they arrived at Shadow Mine?

He knew that Benny and Jasper probably would not bring Dave back to Pine Island. Even if they did, as they had promised, doubtless Dave and he only would be imprisoned again and perhaps in still a worse place than the cold cellar. Getting help was terribly important, the quicker the better, so Dave would have all the more chance to get away safely. After all, Indian Camp wasn't so far, and the Indians had sea skiffs with huge outboard motors and could get word quickly to the police.

Upset now, Pete got up and prowled about the cabin. Perhaps Dave had a chart or a map to help him find his way. He was afraid he might have been mistaken about the exact location of Indian Camp. And again he wished Pine Island wasn't so awfully far up sound. But no need worrying that out again.

He found a few things he could use in the cabin: an extra jacket, a small and slightly dull ax under the sink, a hammer and bag of nails, a small canteen, and, stashed in a corner, a waterproof tarp. But still no map. He opened Dave's desk and thumbed through the papers. There were letters, bills, and lists of numbers that seemed to have no end. There were pencils by the dozens and paper clips and rubber bands. He opened another drawer and saw large envelopes filled with pictures of fish, birds, and animals.

Then he found it, a wonderfully detailed map covering as far north as Swindle Island and south to Namu He brought it back to the fire and spread it out on the rug. Dave's island was on the north side of the sound and, sure enough, Indian Camp was across on the opposite shore. Quickly he measured off the mileage and found to his relief he only would need to go eight miles, plus the distance across the sound itself, which, by using the scale, seemed to be about a mile and a quarter. With luck he could make it. The most dangerous part would be after he passed the point on Pine Island.

Pete folded the map and put it carefully in his pocket. The wind would be a problem, too. If it came up strong and blew against the tide, the chop and swell would be more than the little boat could handle. In that case he would have to beach the boat along the way. And what about the gruesome fog? If it didn't lift, he wouldn't be able even to see the opposite shore. Or what if it came down on him when he was halfway across? At the thought Pete shivered, dreadfully frightened.

He threw more logs on the fire and curled back up in the chair. The fire popped noisily, a cricket chirped cheerily from the stacked wood, and he could smell the sweet scent of pine sap and smoke.

Sleep was the furthest thing from Pete's mind just then. He had to think, to plan. Yet the warmth of the room, the hypnotizing fire, and his worried mind and exhausted body worked against him. Within minutes he was asleep.

CHAPTER 5
Killers on the Sound

Pete was terrified! A massive heaviness was pushing him down, and he could barely breathe. He awoke with a great gasp and clutched for help at the nearest support, the chair. His senses came flying back, and he struggled to shove aside the weight that had stretched out on his chest. It was Crackers, contentedly asleep.

He pushed her roughly to the floor along with her precious bone. "Yick," he said, brushing his sweater with distaste. He went to the window and flung back the curtain. He must have slept past the time he'd planned, but that made little difference just then. What made his heart leap was the sight of a crystal-clear new day.

Quickly he threw the few things he had laid aside the evening before into the waterproof tarp, bundled it into a knot, and rushed out the door. The dew was heavy, and his boots and trouser cuffs were soon wet through.

Crackers bounded along with him. She was so short she had to leap wildly in the air every few feet to see where she was going in the tall grass. They crossed the meadow and ran down the rocky beach.

The boat looked better in the bright light of day. That depressing fog and the shock of what had happened to Dave were behind him now, and he felt more like facing the hours ahead. He unwrapped the tarp and brought out the nails and hammer, then with disgust remembered he had nothing to put over the hole in the boat. Looking around for a piece of wood, Pete saw a dilapidated old shed nearby that once must have been a chicken house. He sorted through the best of its remaining small boards and planks, scraped mud and leaves from one, and nailed it into place. He put the hammer in the boat with the ax and nails and the canteen. Next he shoved the oars in the locks and pushed the boat out from shore.

"Get in, Crackers," he said, and gave the dog a pat. She scrambled in and sat proudly on the seat in the stern as Pete stuffed the tarp in the bow. He would need to hurry, because the tide already was going out, and he must keep it with him the whole distance to Indian Camp. He splashed the oars in the water and took his place. The boat was stable enough, and he was pleased to see there wasn't any water coming in anywhere now that he and Crackers were aboard. He glanced over his shoulder, checked the opposite shore, then the tip of the island, and began to row.

He hadn't gone more than a few strokes when he stopped suddenly and let the oars trail in the water. Of all things, he thought angrily, he had forgotten to pack anything to eat! He hesitated uncertainly. If he took time to bring food from the cabin, he might not make it across with the tide. Yet now he realized he was starved.

"Phooey!" Pete said miserably, turned the boat around again, and started across. His stomach was less important than Dave's safety. Then he noticed Crackers had brought her bone. It was well chewed now and nearly devoured of all parts edible, but she must have felt it still carried some flavor. He thought of having to share it with her and made a face.

The first half of the way Pete managed without trouble, but then he began to get tired. One hand started to hurt, and when he finally stopped for a rest he noticed he had worn a blister. The boat was forever being turned by the tide, and he had to pull much harder to the left. He took off his neckerchief and wrapped it around his hand, then started once more. For a moment he nearly decided to go straight down the middle of the sound with the current. Rowing would be easier, and most probably he would save time in the end. But the security of land close by changed his mind for him, and he headed inshore.

He stopped more often now, readjusting the cloth and wiping perspiration from his forehead. The boat was heavy and awkward and not the least bit easy to move along. He took off his jacket. Crackers settled herself to look at the water over the stern, and Pete went back to work. Lean, pull, lean and pull; he thought his back was going to break. His stomach gurgled emptily, and he began to dream of all the delightful foods he had left behind—the cans of meat, the flour and baking powder just begging him to make them into biscuits. And all those delicious jars of blackberries dripping with syrup. He was perishing with hunger.

Crackers whined and then barked. A sea gull arched overhead and swooped low over the water astern.

"That's just a bird," Pete told her. "Relax. It won't steal your bone." But Crackers jumped across his legs and up to the bow and barked again. Looking far astern, in the distance he saw Pine Island and knew behind the largest stand of trees was the cabin. He was nearly halfway across now and felt as if he had done something really great. For a moment he even began to feel a little smug.

Crackers barked another time. She leaped back over his leg and stood with her paws on the rail, her body quivering with excitement. Pete frowned. She wasn't interested in the bird at all; it was something else. She was looking out over the water, and Pete stopped rowing and leaned on the oars to watch as she growled and shifted about.

Suddenly the glassy smoothness of the sound shattered as if sliced with a dark knife. Pete jerked upright with a start. Spray misted up from the cut water, and he heard a wheeze of exhaled air. Crackers really began to bark then, and Pete watched intently the swirl of water coming in their direction. There was another hiss of air, and he saw yet another fin break the water. Crackers, nearly beside herself, was half out of the boat. Another fin broke the surface. The little dog jumped from thwart to thwart and then to the bow, half arched in a jump ready to leap.

Pete pulled her back by the ears. "You silly mutt," he said lightly. "That's a porpoise come to say hello." Again he heard the hiss of air and off to his right another. "You see, there's a school of them." Now one broke the surface not more than thirty yards away, and he could see the ripple of waves boil away from the fin.

"Maybe it's Flipper. Hey, Flip—" Pete gasped. He grabbed Crackers' harness and yanked her to the bottom of the boat with such a jerk she squealed shrilly.

"Those aren't porpoise!" Pete whispered. He wiped his tongue over his lips while the hair on his neck prickled and stood out. That long, triangular dorsal fin could belong to only one thing—a killer whale! He could count three, perhaps four, and one was so close now that Pete could see the size of its fin. It was huge; the tip towered higher than his own head as he sat in the skiff. Pete swallowed. Crackers barked and tried to break away and leap against the rail. He pressed her tightly in his arms until she was completely still.

Pete never had seen a killer whale so closely before, but he knew of them and their reputation. He had heard shocking stories that made his stomach turn about their unpredictable dispositions. And here he was, a half mile from shore in a flimsy, rickety rowboat that was hardly as much protection as a basket. Dave had told of watching the killers cut a herd of seals to ribbons and destroying schools of salmon they never even attempted to eat. They tore nets to get at fish and nearly demolished the fishermen's boats that tended them.

Now one of the killer whales was coming directly toward him. He could see the wide, glossy back and the white spot around the eye on its head. He dropped Crackers and picked up the oars, which still trailed in the water. If he could get out of its path, it just might pass him by! He strained at the oars with all the strength he owned. The whale changed course the very slightest bit and came straight at him again. Pete pulled powerfully. One oar slipped, noisily popped out of the lock, and clattered along the rail. He snatched it up and put it back into place.

The fin came closer, fifty feet, forty. Pete stared in horror. The killer was longer than the skiff! Its dorsal fin seemed to grow as it came nearer and glistened in the sun like jet.

Then, slowly, the protruding back disappeared, and the fin gradually began to sink beneath the surface. Pete's eyes widened. He could see the hulk of its shape under the crystal water as it came at the boat. He held his breath, waiting for the huge fin to hit the bottom and certainly capsize him. The clear water reflected the sharp bright line between the black of its back and the snowy white of its belly. On its great head he caught the outline of the eye. It was under the boat!

Suddenly the skiff rocked, lurched, and for a sickening second Pete was positive the whale was surfacing under him. But if anything, something worse had happened. Unable to control her enthusiasm, Crackers either had leaped intentionally into the water at the whale or else in her excitement had slipped over by accident.

Pete threw himself toward the bow, crashed over a thwart, and reached for her. She already had surfaced and had begun to swim in a long, arcing turn. But Pete's sudden lurch forward had forced the boat backward and had put just enough distance between them that he was unable to grab her. He looked anxiously underwater, but the dog's splashing dive had rippled the surface so he could see nothing of the killer whale.

"Here, Crackers," he begged, as he stretched his arms toward her, but the distance was still too great. He kneeled in the bow and began to paddle swiftly with his hands, trying to move the boat the few inches closer. Crackers' tail and head were out of the water, and as she swam her paws flashed like pistons. In a second she was nearly close enough to touch, and he strained to reach her again.

Suddenly the water churned and humped; the killer whale's great black fin rose out of the water. It had turned and was coming back!

"Crackers!" Pete sobbed. But she was not interested. She turned toward the killer whale without the slightest concern. Pete lunged to his feet, ripped one of the trailing oars out of the lock and threw it spear-fashion at the fin. It hit the water to the left of the whale, and by the time he had the second oar in his hand the distance between whale and dog had halved. Pete flung the other oar. It skimmed the surface, and though it did not deter the whale it did succeed thoroughly in frightening Crackers. She turned about instantly and headed toward the boat.

Now the fin flashed through the water at twice its former speed, and the monster slowly rolled to one side as it came up on the dog. Once more Pete hastily paddled the boat with his hands. Crackers glanced over her shoulder and for a moment nearly turned back to face the killer another time. Pete strained forward, touched her, then clutched her by the harness. There was a heaving rush of water, and the great fin cut in a sharp turn beside the boat. Pete saw the white underside of the whale as it came at him—its gaping mouth, the teeth!

He screamed and fell into the bottom of the boat with his hands over his head in horror. The skiff rolled violently, water gushed over the rail, drenching him, and he gripped the splintery floorboards with all his strength.

Then he heard Crackers bark. He had flung the dog into the boat after all, and now she was up, dancing around the thwart with as much excitement as ever. He reached up and yanked her sharply into the bottom of the skiff just as another flood of water rolled over the rail and the boat rocked dangerously near capsizing. He clutched the dog to his chest, clamped her mouth tightly shut, and pressed himself low. He heard the roar of exhaled air as the whale breathed, and Pete closed his eyes, expecting the end.

Again the boat rolled and danced on its beam-ends, while he heard another hiss of breathing and felt the nearness of the monster. He wondered hopelessly if it could rear up, look over the rail, and see him huddled terrified in the bottom. Another rasp of air. Was it farther away? They were rolling less. He loosened his grip around Crackers' jaws, and she wiggled restlessly. Now the boat was sitting quietly, with hardly the slightest motion.

Pete opened his eyes. He focused on the pinkish white barrenness of Crackers' well-chewed bone. It was no more than three inches from his nose, and it sent him into a spasm of shivering, caused purely from fright. He raised his eyes and saw the blue of sky. Cautiously he pulled himself up farther and peered over the rail. The water was as silver smooth as glass. Overhead, the sea gull winged slowly back toward land. He sat up, still holding Crackers immobile. Far, far in the distance he saw the killer whales and the water cut by their fins as they swam together heading up sound.

Pete bent his head and rested it prayerfully on Crackers' back. He took a deep and rather ragged breath to steady himself, for he well knew they were lucky still to be alive.

Then with a jolt he realized how badly Crackers smelled. She was very wet, and her long hair looked like strips of tarred cord. And now he was wet, and the boat nearly was swamped. He let her go, and she wagged her moplike tail eagerly.

The first thing was to get the water out of the boat. Pete cupped his hands and tried to scoop it out. That method didn't work, so he pulled off his hat and bailed with it. Every few minutes he glanced up to check the course of the whales. They were nearly out of sight now and very hard to see.

Pete straightened up and sucked in his breath sharply. The reason they were hard to see was because the fog was coming in. He dropped his hat and scrambled to his place on the thwart. Then with a frantic gasp he pressed his hands over his mouth in horror. The oars! He had thrown them at the whale! Panicked, he looked around the horizon, and to his immense relief he saw them about forty feet away. He leaped into the bow and began paddling with his hands. No matter about the whales now! If he lost those oars in the fog, the current would take him right out to sea, and that truly would be the end. Already the fog had blotted out Dave's island. In another ten minutes it would be as thick as cotton.

He reached the oars and pulled them aboard thankfully. With a clatter he shoved them into the locks. The fog, the tide, the whales—everything was against him. He had to get closer to the beach before he lost his bearings completely. Already a smoky sort of haze covered the world around him. A breeze rippled the sound, as cat's-paws came toward him ahead of the fog. He rowed furiously. Crackers settled down on the stern seat and yawned.

"You—you—" Now that fear was past, Pete felt only anger. Crackers put her head on her paws and looked up at him with sorrowful eyes. "Yes nearly got yourself eaten," he told her shortly.

By the time they finally reached shore, the fog had settled in thickly, but Pete felt so sure he could make Indian Camp despite the poor visibility he kept right on. Besides, he knew if he stopped rowing he soon would be chilled to the bone, for he was soaking wet. And he did not at all like the thought of spending a night on the forbidding, deserted shoreline. He threw the tarp over his legs, for what warmth it might give, and settled down for another long session at the oars.

His course kept him quite close to the rocks, but there was no surf on this side of the sound. After his experience with the whales, he wanted to be very near land if they should reappear. He was also afraid that if he strayed far from shore he accidentally might pass Indian Camp in the fog.

For a long while it seemed he was destined to be alone forever. He could see nothing except the shrouded skiff and the hazy patch of shoreline he kept barely within sight. Even Crackers had disappeared. She had snuggled beneath the canvas and was fast asleep.

Might he have misjudged his distances? Could he already have passed the settlement? His loneliness filled him with a dreadful sense of foreboding. Wild and hopeless thoughts tormented him. Yet he rowed on, knowing in his heart he was not the last remaining person on earth.

CHAPTER 6

Indian Camp

The first sound, other than the rattle and squeak of the oars, came much later. At first he thought he had imagined it, but Crackers squirmed out from under the tarp sleepily, one ear cocked at attention. Pete stopped rowing and felt the ache in his arms and back swell like fire. Crackers whined.

"Shhh!" Pete hissed. Faintly, he heard it again—the distant bark of a dog. The crispness of a wood fire somewhere near came to him, mingled with the green smell of tide-exposed rocks. His heart leaped with excitement, and quickly he went back to the oars. Within minutes the hazy outline of fishing nets, hung between poles to dry, hove into view. The dock was ahead, and with a sudden spurt of energy Pete speeded the last few yards.

He made a noisy, bumpy landing on the pier and tied the skiff with a frayed line hanging from a piling. As he climbed to the dock, he found he was so painfully stiff he could hardly stand upright. Crackers jumped out nimbly and disappeared up a path and into the fog. Pete stretched his back, then leaned forward and peered into the mists at the rest of the dock. Where were all the boats? When Dave and he had landed last spring, the dock had been crowded to overflowing. Could he have landed at the wrong place?

Pete turned hastily and started up the path. It was slippery with mud, and Crackers bounded back to lead his way. Everything looked ghostly in the fog, and deserted; it all nearly unnerved him. Crackers disappeared again, and in a moment, much to his genuine relief, a voice called out.

"Hello," he called back.

"Hallo! You Davey there?" It was an Indian woman, as ancient as the hills. She wore a long and rather poorly fitting brown dress, and a plastic raincoat was thrown over her shoulders.

"Hello," Pete repeated stupidly.

"Biscuits here," she said in a croaking, hoarse voice. "Biscuits come say hi-hi."

For a moment Pete felt as if he were going to burst into tears. She was staring at him queerly, and Pete realized he must look a bit peculiar. He was soaking wet, and his bailing cap drooped on his head like a wet rag. The tarpaulin was under his arm, the ax and hammer in his hand. The canteen was slung around his neck, and it hung down like a giant medallion.

"I—I'm looking for help," he said to her.

"You not Davey," she noted thoughtfully. "Where Davey? Biscuits here."

"Dave was taken prisoner by two men in a helicopter," Pete blurted out.

She came nearer and peered at him carefully. She was very slight in build and looked like a wizened old witch. "You sure not Davey," she wheezed. "How come you got Biscuits?"

"You mean Crackers," said Pete, realizing at last that she was talking about the dog.

"Biscuits, crackers. All same me."

Pete breathed unsteadily. "Please, I must get help. I must get to the police in Bella Bella."

She cackled like an old hen. "You small boy with crazy head."

"Grandmother! You should not say things like that." Pete swung around and faced the young woman who came out of the fog like a wraith. "Hello," she went on in a sweet, musical voice to Pete. "I don't know you, do I?"

He shook his head. "I'm Pete Fleming," he explained. "I've been staying with my brother on Pine Island."

She came closer and looked at his wet mackinaw. "Yes. I know Dave Fleming. Is something wrong?"

"Oh," Pete gasped. "Oh, yes. It's Dave." She nodded with understanding. "Two men landed and—"

"Wait." The young woman held out her hand. "First

let us go inside." She turned to another woman who came out of the mists. "He is tired and very wet. Perhaps your Steven's clothes will fit him. Come." She turned back to Pete, and he stumbled after her into a small cabin.

A baby, sitting beside a table in a high chair, stopped spooning food into his mouth to stare at Pete. Another child sat on a long bench and whacked a cup against her dish impatiently. In a minute a woman appeared with dry clothing and showed him to a room in which to change. When he returned to join them, he sat exhausted in a straight-backed chair drawn up to the scrubbed table. A small boy handed him a bowl of meaty stew and slabs of hard bread and cheese. Pete was so hungry he nearly swallowed it all in one gulp.

The same young woman who had seemed to understand he had a very great problem put her hand on his shoulder and smiled. "My name is Ellen Snowflower."

"How do you do?" Pete said politely.

"Now, Pete," she said gently, as the boy refilled his dish, "while you eat, start from the very beginning, please, and tell us exactly what has happened."

And he did, from the time the men had arrived in the helicopter until the moment he had stood before her. Every few minutes during his recitation she held up her hand, halting him, and turning to the gathering group of women and children who kept coming in the cabin door repeated in Indian what he had said. When he came to the part about the killer whales, he saw the look of horror quickly cross their faces. The Indians knew these deadly visitors of the sound very well indeed.

"And you have come all this way in Dave's old boat?"

Pete nodded.

"You are very brave," the young woman said. Pete shook his head. "But you are," she went on gravely, "to think first of your brother."

"The police can get up to Shadow Mountain with the helicopter stationed at Bella Bella," Pete said quickly. "They can get Dave away from those two."

She nodded. Another woman asked a question, and she translated. "Mrs. Moonstone asks if you or your brother were hurt?"

Pete thought for a moment. "Dave probably has a sore head."

"Ah," said the young woman, "but he is very tough."

Pete went on hurriedly. "What are we going to do? Can we get word down to Bella Bella by boat in this fog?"

She was sitting in a chair beside him, and Pete watched as she clasped her hands together softly, then rested them on her knees. She pursed her lips, and Pete felt a welling of fear creep over him.

"No. That will be impossible." She looked around the room at the kind and sincere faces of the listening women and children. "We are alone here."

"The boats!" asked Pete hoarsely. "The sea skiffs with the big motors!"

"Ah," she said, closing her eyes briefly. "But now there are none at all.

"The salmon are running," explained Ellen Snowflower. "It is as simple as that."

Pete stared at her. "But the boats? Will they be back?"

She nodded her dark head. "Yes. But not until the fishing has begun to slacken. Even then our menfolk stop to unload the catch at the cannery in Bella Bella before they come home."

"Will they be back tomorrow?" he asked quickly.

"No. Probably not until next week. Perhaps not even then." She touched his arm lightly. "I am very sorry. We are all very good friends of your brother's, and we want just as much as you to help."

Pete put his head in his hands hopelessly. His effort to reach Indian Camp apparently had been for nothing. The baby beside him flicked applesauce on his high chair and smeared it with a pudgy hand. "But we must get help," Pete said anxiously.

"Of course. And I have been thinking about it. Do you know of the Indian Camp Guide Service and the man who runs it?"

"No," said Pete, "but can he help us?"

Ellen Snowflower nodded. "I believe so. He is a guide, you know, and takes people out hunting and fishing in the bush. He hasn't a boat, but he does have a truck, though I don't believe it would be of much use. Ocean Falls is so far away, and, of course, it is impossible to get over to Bella Bella without a boat or a plane. But he does have a radio transmitter."

She stood up quickly. "Yes, I'm sure he is our answer. He can call the police for us."

CHAPTER 7

Jackstraw

Pete was on his feet instantly.

"I will take you down to his cabin myself," she went on. "He sometimes seems a bit gruff to strangers. Besides, he is my uncle."

Pete already had gathered up the tarp and slung the canteen back over his neck. "May I wear these clothes until I get back?"

"Of course." She turned to the women and spoke to them rapidly in Indian, and they nodded in agreement. The old crone he first had met in the fog punched him gently with her cane.

"Look like Indian boy, for sure," she cackled cheerfully.

Pete guessed he did at that, as he examined his borrowed sweater. Only the Indians wore the heavy woolen ones knitted with strange designs. His was covered with beaked birds with popping eyes.

Ellen put on a raincoat and tied a flowered scarf over her head. "It is about a mile," she said. "You must be tired after so long a row. Are you sure you want to come?"

"Yes," said Pete. "That meal fixed me up right." He looked at her gravely. "Thank you very much."

Ellen smiled. "But you are most welcome. Come now, we will take the inland trail because it is the quickest."

There was still thick, drippy fog outside, and the women and children followed them as far as the clearing before waving good-bye. Crackers bounced out of the mists followed by a tiny, barrel-shaped puppy, which Ellen shooed back toward camp.

They walked quickly, and after the first few minutes Pete was so thoroughly lost he never would have been able to find his way out alone. They were in dense forest and were following a path thickly covered with slippery pine needles. It was very still, the only sound the soft pad of their muffled footsteps. They could see but a few feet around them, and the grass and trees were wet and dark-looking. There was no sign of the sun; the world was a dreary, leaden gray.

They met no one along the way. A bird thrashed out of the brambles once, and later they saw a squirrel jitter up and around a tree. At one place the path through the growth was so narrow they had to turn sideways to scrape by, and then the dew spattered down on them like rain. As they approached a slight clearing, a sudden explosion of wings caused Pete nearly to collide into Ellen as she came to an abrupt halt. But it was only a covey of quail, and they skittered and glided into the thickest brush.

"Goodness," said Ellen. "I didn't see them."

Crackers barked shrilly and started to give chase, but Pete lunged, caught her harness, and dragged her along unwillingly.

"Come on," he said between his teeth. "Can't you ever mind your own simple business?"

A few minutes later Ellen exclaimed breathlessly, "Here we are."

A cabin had appeared before them as if by some sleight of hand. Their trek through the trees had brought them out onto the shore of the sound once again, for Pete could hear the faint lap of waves along the rocks. Ellen pounded on the door with the flat of her hand, and in a moment it opened.

"Hello, Uncle," she said brightly. Pete stared at the man, stunned. He had expected to see an Indian, or at least someone who looked like an Indian. This man had red hair and a great red moustache, which hung down in a big loop on each side of his lips. "I've brought a friend," Ellen went on. "There's been trouble over at Pine Island."

The man motioned them inside. "Dave sick?" he asked bluntly.

"Oh, goodness no," said Ellen quickly. "Dave Fleming has been kidnapped."

"Kidnapped!" Pete saw he had certainly gotten a jolt from that news.

Ellen nodded, took a seat at a roughhewn log table, and told the story quickly. When she finished, the man turned to Pete sharply.

"So you crossed the sound, eh?"

Pete nodded.

"And you ran into killer whales?"

"Yes, sir."

"And you let that dog of Dave's leap out and try and retrieve you one, eh?"

Pete licked his lips. "Well—I—"

"Mighty stupid," he said shortly. "Dog that dumb, you should of let it get eaten."

Pete flushed. As if he ever would have let any dog be eaten alive if he could help it.

Ellen was smiling slightly, as if she was accustomed to her uncle's brusqueness. Pete thought he was being frightfully rude and not at all nice.

"What is it you want me to do?" he growled at Pete. "Shave it off?"

Pete started and looked down at his hands in embarrassment. He had been staring at the man's moustache as if mesmerized. It was the most fascinating thing he had ever seen.

"I suppose you want to use the radio," he said to Ellen, and when she nodded, he pulled a cover from a set on top of a tall chest. It looked complicated to operate. "Won't do you any good, though."

"What do you mean?" said Pete angrily. "Don't you believe me?"

The man fiddled with the set, twisted dials, and snapped a switch. "Sure, I believe you. But you see, I just got a call from the constable in Bella Bella about an hour ago. He mentioned their helicopter was in Bella Coola having an overhaul."

"Oh," said Pete. "Oh, no."

The man nodded. "It was sent up from Bella Bella two days ago."

"Can't they get another?" asked Ellen.

Her uncle grunted slightly. "They haven't been able to get one from Bella Coola or even Ocean Falls, because all the planes were needed for the big fire over near Kimsquit." His sharp eyes bored into Pete's, thinking out the dilemma. "I'll give a call now and see what the constable wants to do." He stroked his moustache absently. "Fine thing. Friend of mine in trouble and no way to help." Then he clapped his hands briskly and said, "Well, let's get busy."

Pete leaped to his feet, eager to be of assistance. The man adjusted earphones over his head and flicked another switch, which suddenly glowed red. "Say, I don't even know your name," the man said.

Ellen gasped. "My manners are terrible. Pete Fleming, meet Jackstraw."

Pete shook hands solemnly.

"Mine's an Indian name," Jackstraw said conversationally. "You think I'm an Indian?" Pete hesitated.

"Well, I am." Then he added with a chuckle, "Though my mother just happened to be Irish. Say, did you see that totem out in front of my house?"

"No."

"Belonged to my grandfather," he went on pleasantly, as he adjusted more dials. "It's one of the only old totems left in Canada, except those down in Victoria. They tried to get my totem away from me, but I wouldn't sell it for a million dollars. Well now, maybe for a million dollars I would at that." Then he spoke into the transmitter and contacted the constable in Bella Bella.

And he had been right. There was no helicopter for the authorities to use and get help to Dave. In fact, things began to look very bleak indeed until the constable hit upon an idea that seemed to meet with Jackstraw's approval. After he shut down the set, he outlined the plan for Ellen and Pete.

"I'll take the truck as far as the river and meet Constable Perry and two of his men at the cliffs. They have a high-speed launch, and though they will need to cover a lot of miles, I ought to arrive there at about the same time."

"Is it so awfully far?" Pete asked hesitantly. "To Shadow Mountain?"

Jackstraw scratched his chin. "Well, no. From here it's about twenty miles. But the constable has to take his boat up sound, pass Pine Island, and go beyond about twenty miles to the Kilpatrick River. It's navigable, and he can shoot up it for another thirty-five miles and meet me without ever having to set foot ashore. I'd go that way myself—it's a mighty rough trek by land—but"—he ran his finger along his moustache unconsciously—"I haven't a boat, and that high-speed launch of the constable's would be far too overloaded for me and all the gear I need to take."

"Will you guide them up the difficult part of the mountain?" asked Ellen.

Jackstraw nodded. "I know the way well enough."

"When will you leave?" Pete demanded quickly.

"Right away. We won't get help to Dave as fast as by using a plane, but I can get them on the summit by tomorrow afternoon." He stroked his moustache again. "All things willing, that is."

Pete rubbed his palms together nervously. "Please, may I go?"

Jackstraw looked at him thoughtfully. "No," he said finally. "You can stay with Ellen and her family. I can take you over to Bella Bella when everything's over."

"Over," said Pete. "Over! But it's Dave! Besides"—he stood up angrily, his fists clenched—"I've a right to go."

"Oh?" said Jackstraw lightly. "And why do you think you have any right to do a man's work?"

"Because Dave is my brother, that's why, and I'm the one who told you. If I hadn't come this far, you'd still not know what had happened to him. I'm entitled to go!"

"He has got a point," said Ellen in his defense. "He may only be a boy, but he seems to have done rather well so far."

Jackstraw shrugged. "It will be a rough trip and a fast one."

Pete sucked in his breath. "I can manage," he said, with a grateful glance at Ellen.

She smiled. "Personally, I think you are unwise to go along. But I have two brothers, and I understand perfectly."

"Well, don't just stand there," said Jackstraw. "If you're going, tote that gear by the door out to the truck, and let's get under way." He already had slipped off his moccasins and was lacing up his heavy boots. By the time Pete had carried the duffle bag and one box to the truck and returned, Jackstraw had collected more gear and was pulling on his jacket. "Better take this," he said, tossing him an extra mackinaw. "And this poncho. It's going to be wet."

"I'm loading the food box," Ellen said, as she collected edibles from the kitchen shelves.

Jackstraw motioned Pete to take four coils of line and a belt of rings and metal spikes. "Put those in the back seat." Pete nodded and on the way stopped for a moment to look at the huge totem pole that stood on the edge of the cleared yard. The grotesque, painted faces looked frightening as they glared out of the fog above him. When he came back in the house, Jackstraw was taking a rifle from above the mantel.

"This thing was meant purely as decoration," he said half to himself. "It's a rusty mess." Pete looked at the antique gun. It certainly wasn't what he would call in very good shape. This thought must have occurred to Jackstraw, because he turned and glared at Pete unnecessarily. "All my guns are down in Courtenay. I send them in this time every year and have them checked over. Don't think this is my way of taking care of firearms!" He handed the gun to Pete with a growl. "It might scare somebody, but that's all it's good for."

"Jasper and Benny have guns," Pete said cautiously. "One's a shotgun, and the other is a hand gun."

"Well, I don't plan ever to get close enough to see them. My job is just to get the constable up there."

Pete hardly knew what to make of the man. It was impossible to tell if he was serious or not. He strapped the gun on the rifle rack across the back window of the truck. It certainly did not look very impressive. Then Jackstraw came out carrying more gear and the camp box, and he gave Ellen a hasty kiss on the cheek.

Suddenly Pete remembered Crackers. She was playfully worrying his trouser cuff and making wet, growling noises while her tail thumped the grass. "What will I do about her?"

Jackstraw gave the dog a friendly scratch on the head. "Crackers, the whale bait," he said, and let her smother him with licks of her tongue. "Ellen can keep her till we get back."

Pete nodded reluctantly. No need asking if he could

take her along, he was lucky to be able to go himself.
He patted Crackers good-bye, then slipped a piece of
cord on her harness.

"I'll take good care of her," said Ellen, taking the
makeshift leash. "Don't worry."

Jackstraw swung to the driver's seat, and Pete scrambled in beside him. There was no door, and Jackstraw
leaned over and snapped a safety strap across the gaping space where it ought to have been. As he started
the motor with a roar, Pete felt a tingle of excitement.
They waved to Ellen while Crackers strained to get free
and come along. Then Jackstraw swung the wheel, and
they bumped down the gravelly, rutted trail that served
as a road.

CHAPTER 8

Swamped

For the first few minutes Pete assumed the horrible track was merely an unused byroad into Jackstraw's cabin. Instead of improving, however, it steadily got worse, and Pete hung on with both hands to keep from being thrown bodily out into the brush. He doubted if the road ever had seen the likes of a bulldozer's blade or a grader. It seemed simply to be an animal trail, widened by Jackstraw's truck as it beat through on rare occasions.

There was too much noise to talk. The truck was in compound low, and whined and growled like an enraged lion. Rocks and sticks and all sorts of debris shot up underneath and rattled and crashed on the metal. When they came to the narrower parts, they scraped through with a squeak of limbs scratching against the body. The windshield was brown with mud, left there from some other time, and the cleared patches made by the wipers seemed like two eyes. The spare tire mounted on the hood was caked with mud and looked as if it, too, had been well used.

"Wouldn't exactly call this a Rolls," Jackstraw shouted at him. "But it sure"—they crashed into a pothole, and the truck lunged violently to one side —"gets me there."

Pete nodded and wondered what was going to happen up ahead. For the past half hour they had followed a twisting, raging river that Jackstraw called the Little Qualicum, and now the path went directly across it. It didn't look especially shallow and was white with rapids. They pulled up at the edge of the water and squeaked to a rocking halt.

"Blast and double blast," grumbled Jackstraw. "Must be having a soaker up in the mountains."

"We can't get across," said Pete miserably. When Jackstraw turned to look at him a little impatiently, he went on. "Well, can we?"

"We sure enough are going to try. First get all this stuff up off the floor, front and back. The extra fuel cans are all right; the water won't come up over their tops. Besides, I think Tilly here runs on half water."

Pete pulled the gear higher on the seats. "But won't the water hurt the engine?" he asked.

"Exhaust is mounted overhead," Jackstraw explained. "It probably isn't that deep anyway. All ready?"

"I—I guess," Pete said uncertainly, as they began to

inch into the boiling water. Almost immediately they dropped off a shelf with a great lurch, and water bubbled over the door lip. Pete jerked his feet up on the seat to escape getting wet. "Yikes!" he gasped.

The engine groaned in protest, and Jackstraw struggled with the steering. The boulders in the stream bed were large and loose, and they threw the wheels first to one side and then the other. The water got deeper, too. Jackstraw's feet disappeared and then his ankles. Next the motor coughed and stopped.

"Charming, charming," Jackstraw said unpleasantly, as he ground the starter over and over without the slightest success. "So now we're stuck."

Pete chewed at his lip. "What'll we do?"

"Get out of the creek first thing," the man answered shortly. "It would have to be flooding right now."

"Will the water get higher?" Pete asked, alarmed.

Jackstraw shrugged, then as if he parked in midriver every day of his life, he stepped out nonchalantly into water hip-deep. "Well, come on, boy. Don't be a freeloader."

Pete dropped his feet off the seat and into the water. So much for trying to keep them dry any longer. He pulled off his sweaters and stuffed them into the gun rack. He was on the downstream side of the current, and he stepped into the water gingerly.

"Brr!" he said, as the water came up over his waist. "It's cold!"

"Pure ice cubes," agreed Jackstraw, as Pete stum-

bled over to him. Keeping his balance in the swift current was difficult, and he held onto the slippery metal
so as not to get swept away. Jackstraw was bent over
the front of the truck, his hands working beneath the
surface. Suddenly he pulled the end of a steel cable out
of the water and handed it to Pete. "We'll have to
winch her out," he explained. "Take this over to one
of those big pines, and secure it."

Pete took the metal hook and staggered toward
shore. Pulling the cable off its reel, which was attached
to the front of the bumper, was very awkward. When
he stumbled into the grass, he found the sturdiest of
the trees, looped the cable around, then slipped the
hook into it again. "All set!" he called back to Jackstraw. The man nodded, and Pete waded back through
the water to help.

"I've put the handle in the winch," Jackstraw said,
straightening up. "It's not hard to turn, but give it a
try."

Pete thrust his arms into the cold, murky water and
felt along the bumper to the bulky windlass. He found
the protruding handle on one end and turned it.

"All right?" asked Jackstraw.

Pete nodded.

"Okay, then I'll push and try to steer." He splashed
off, and Pete began reeling in.

The work was easy enough, for the winch was geared
down considerably, but it seemed forever before the
truck moved forward. When it did, the wheels whipped

violently from side to side, and Jackstraw struggled to keep them in line.

Pete stooped uncomfortably over the crank as he wound in cable. Water splashed in his face, boulders rolled under his feet, and some sort of black gnats buzzed around his eyes irritably. But, most of all, his body ached from the freezing water.

Suddenly something nudged him on the back! It wasn't a log floating downstream or anything like that. It was alive, and he could hear it breathe. He let out a shriek, let the winch go, and flung himself toward Jackstraw.

The man looked up startled, "What—"

"S—something tried to bite me," Pete choked. "There!" He saw an animal swimming toward him, and again he lunged toward the truck ready to climb inside for what protection it would give. But Jackstraw took his arm firmly and shook his head slightly. His expression brought Pete to a halt, and he looked at the beast a little more closely.

"It's Crackers!" he said, stunned.

The little dog was battling the current bravely, and now she came up to Pete once more and nudged him gently with her nose. He caught her up and held her squirming in his arms as she licked at his face happily.

"I thought Ellen was going to take care of her," Jackstraw said in exasperation. Then he fingered the broken and frayed cord used as her leash. "Just what we need is a wet dog."

Pete pushed Crackers on the truck seat and hurried back to his work. Obviously Crackers had broken away without much trouble, and though he hoped her disappearance wouldn't worry Ellen Snowflower, secretly he was delighted the dog was with them. They had been moving as slow as snails over the bad road, and being swamped in the stream had given her plenty of time to catch up.

In a moment the dog leaped back out of the truck and swam to Pete. He grinned. She was an awful pest. She splashed him in the face and scratched her claws on his arm for attention. But each time he returned her to the front seat, she swam back.

"She's half fish," said Jackstraw, as he caught her by the tail on her last dive and tossed her back in the truck ungracefully. The next moment the truck wobbled out onto the shore. Quickly Jackstraw set the emergency brake, and for a moment they stared at the dripping truck. Crackers barked and leaped to the ground, dancing wildly around Pete, ready to play.

Jackstraw flipped up the hood and looked at the engine. Water ran off it in rivulets, and though he tried time and again it still would not start.

"Get the camp box unloaded," he told Pete finally. "And set up the primus."

Pete sorted through the boxes on the seats. They all had stayed perfectly dry, and he carried the one he wanted to a stump and put it down. The stove was in a small tin box, and he had lived and camped with his brother long enough to know how to assemble it. First he took out the round tank no larger than his cupped hands and folded out three small legs. Next he screwed in the burner, pushed in three steel rods to hold up the burner, and adjusted the grill on it. He put the wind screen in place and took out the priming can.

"Start it up," Jackstraw said. He had a small, black, tube-shaped part of the engine in his hand.

Pete filled the priming cup and lit the alcohol. "What's that?" he asked, pointing to the object in Jackstraw's hand.

"The coil. We can bake it out for a while. It looks wet." He turned and looked at Pete. "You'd better get into some dry clothes."

Pete hesitated. "I don't have any," he said finally. "Everything is at Dave's cabin."

"Hmm. Well, look through my duffle and see if you can find some extra trousers, and get out a pair for me." He gave the stove a pump, and it roared into life. He tied the coil to a branch and propped it up near the heat. "I'll wipe off the ignition system," he said, as he ripped a section of dry cloth from a rag he had found in the camp box. "How about starting up a fire and try drying out our clothes?"

Pete found the pants and once into them searched about for dry wood. His wet boots bothered him the most. They squished. Soon enough he found that getting a big fire going was easy, but he had trouble with the tripods of sticks he built to hold their wet things.

Every time Pete got the clothes stretched out on them, either they fell down of their own accord or else Crackers stalked the wet pieces and dragged them off through the dirt like captured prey. He put their boots on long poles and propped them over the fire where they steamed and sizzled cheerfully. He considered putting on a pot of water for tea, then decided he might not have the time, for Jackstraw had cleaned up the motor and had just finished bailing out the remaining water standing inside the cab. Nearly a half hour had passed since they were stranded. Jackstraw looked up and asked Pete to bring the coil so he could bolt it back into place.

The work was interesting to Pete. He did not know much about cars or trucks, but he tried to hand Jackstraw the proper tools as he needed them. "What's that?" he asked, and pointed at another engine part with its top hanging off to one side. It was obviously drying out like everything else.

"The distributor," said Jackstraw, and snapped the cap back into place. "Well, I'll give her a try." He slid into the front seat and in a moment the starter ground over with a whine, the motor coughed, and started up.

"You fixed it," Pete said with admiration.

Jackstraw grinned and revved the motor furiously. "Put away the stove, and I'll douse that fire."

Pete ran to pack the hot primus. He wadded the nearly dried clothes into a box and slipped on his boots. They were hot, and he danced about as if he were walking on coals.

Jackstraw began shoveling dirt onto the fire, and Pete ran back and forth with the water bucket to drench the last of it. Crackers followed and nipped playfully at his heels.

"That's it," said Jackstraw, as he strapped the shovel on the fender. Pete hastily shoved the camp box in the back and quickly climbed into the already moving Tilly.

CHAPTER 9

A Narrow Escape

"Are there any more places like that to ford?" Pete asked, as they bumped off down the track once again.

"No more creeks," Jackstraw shouted back, and shoved Crackers to one side with his elbow. "But there is a river."

Pete pulled the dog down on the seat. She was licking Jackstraw on the ear with affectionate swipes. "Do you mean *that* wasn't a river?"

"Nope."

"Will it be flooding, too?" he asked.

Jackstraw shifted down and the truck growled throatily. "Probably. The water all comes from the same place."

"Glick!" said Pete.

"But don't worry," Jackstraw offered. "There's a ferry for that one."

Pete heaved a sigh of relief and tugged Crackers

back from Jackstraw again, holding her clamped in his arms. Never in his life had he seen such a squirmy dog.

"Road's better now," Jackstraw announced. "There's a lumber camp up country, and the trucks have kept this part in pretty fair shape."

Pete wasn't impressed. To him, the track seemed as rough as ever. They had been climbing steadily and very steeply, and now he began to wonder why the truck didn't flip end over end. He hung on nervously. The fog had become so thick they could see only a few feet ahead.

Suddenly there was a thrash of underbrush beside the truck. Pete started violently as two moose leaped directly across in front of them. Jackstraw whipped the wheel to one side and slammed his foot on the brake. But not quickly enough. His violent turn had crashed them into a tree, dead center.

Crackers barked furiously, leaped across the seat, and out after the disappearing animals. Pete lunged for her, missed, lost his balance, and tumbled headfirst out the door and into the brush.

"For crying out loud!" Jackstraw shouted at him, and killed the engine. Pete picked himself up off the ground, but the dog already had run into the fog. "Don't go chasing after her," Jackstraw went on irritably, as he tried to restart the engine. "If she doesn't come back, she can spend the rest of her life right here. Come on, come on, you stupid truck," he growled, "you're temperamental as some prima donna."

Pete grinned. The truck ought to be moody, considering its hard life. He whistled for Crackers. Somewhere, in the far distance, he could hear her bark, but she obviously was going away from them. Jackstraw was still grumbling, and Pete wandered around to look at the front end. The truck hadn't suffered any apparent damage from its head-on collision, but the foot-thick tree was a goner. It had cracked off about bumper height.

"Don't back up," Pete said quickly, as the motor roared into life. "If you do, this tree is going to come crashing down on top of you."

Jackstraw got out and came to look at their risky position. "Go get one of those coils of line out of the back," he ordered, and gave a push at the offending tree. It creaked over him more precariously than ever, and he stepped back hastily. Pete handed him the line.

"This might work," he said, tossing the rope over a limb as far up in the tree as he could, then letting it fall to the ground. He slipped a knot into the end, looked at the surrounding trees, saw one that seemed to fit his need, and tied the bitter end as tightly around it as he could. "That ought to hold it up until I can get the truck out of there. But stand back. Sometimes my ideas don't work out quite as planned."

"Be careful," Pete said uneasily. "If that line breaks, the tree will fall right on you."

Jackstraw climbed in the truck and began to move it backward. With each inch the tree teetered downward

a little more, until the dacron line took up slack and became so tight it twanged like a guitar string. Pete pushed his hands over his lips. Now the truck was away, and the thin line held the entire weight of the split tree. Jackstraw reversed violently, and in his rush to get out from under nearly disappeared from sight in the fog. Pete let out his breath in relief.

"Now to get my line back all in one piece," Jackstraw said. He stroked his moustache thoughtfully and examined the precariously leaning tree.

"Can't you just release the line?" Pete asked. "And let the whole thing crash down?"

Jackstraw frowned. "Well, I suppose. But keep behind me. Once I let go of this end, it will come down like a lead balloon." Slowly and carefully he began to let out the knot that held the weight of the pine. At that moment a piercing howl rent the air.

"Crackers!" Pete choked, and started for the dog as she bumbled happily out of the brush directly beneath the tree.

"Watch it!" Jackstraw grabbed his arm, holding him back. The line was beyond stopping now.

"No! Oh, no!" Pete screamed at Crackers. "Go back!"

Suddenly Jackstraw moved like the wind, without the slightest heed of the tree that already had begun to topple. He leaped under the splintering pine and gave Crackers a kick in the rump that sent her yelping safely into the brush.

Now the tree's angle was so great it came crashing through the other trees with a tearing and ripping of branches. Jackstraw made a wild half twist of his body and threw himself in a great lunge as far away as he could get before the tree hit the ground with a thunderous roar.

There was a wild swaying and settling of the pine's smaller branches, and the stirred ground cover settled back to earth. The only sound now was the soft drip of dew from the trees and the faint click of the truck engine as it idled nearby.

"Jackstraw," Pete whispered, and dove into the thick branches, spreading them apart with his hands. "Jackstraw!"

Crackers bounded out of the mists and barked shrilly. She shoved her way into the pine needles and playfully caught Pete's pant's cuff and tugged it. "Jackstraw!" Pete called hysterically.

"Okay. I'm okay, Pete," the man's voice answered from somewhere beneath the greenery.

Jackstraw's hand came up through the limbs as he clutched for a handhold. When he stood up, miraculously he was all in one piece. Pete took a long, steadying breath. There was a sweet smell of bruised pine, and his hands felt sticky with sap where he had clutched the bark of the tree with a grip of iron.

"Man, I could kill that dog," Jackstraw said angrily, as he climbed out of the branches and glared down at Crackers. But she only jumped up affectionately on his leg and barked cheerfully. "She has all the brains of a lower-class stump."

"Are you all right?" Pete asked, getting his voice back into shape.

"Sure. I'm used to having trees fall on top of me." He clapped Pete on the shoulder and smoothed his ruffled red moustache back into place. "Well, let's get started again. It's getting late, and I'd sure like to get across the river before dark."

They climbed back in the truck, Crackers between them, and she panted and drooled on their hands. Pete held her harness firmly. "Is it much farther?" he asked, as they crept up the hill.

"Not much. It's over this ridge and then down to the bottom of the valley. In fact, I guess this is the summit now. It's hard to see in this blooming fog."

"Yeee!" exclaimed Pete, as the truck lurched over the top of the hill and dropped off the other side. The front end pointed nearly straight down, and the back wheels skidded on the rocks and slippery pine needles. The boxes and gear in the back crashed off the seat onto the floor, and the duffle bag tumbled into the front, burying Crackers beneath it.

"One thing about going downhill," Jackstraw said between his teeth as he fought the skid, "you don't waste any time."

Pete pushed his shoulder against the windshield and his hands against the dash. They skidded again, and now Pete could see the roadbed had turned to slimy mud. Jackstraw swung the wheel with wild turns of his arms, and Pete felt sure he would lose control and they would pivot about completely. Yet somehow he kept them pointed in the proper direction, and in just a few minutes the hill smoothed out, and they slid to a stop.

"There!" breathed Jackstraw, and laid a heavy hand on the horn. Crackers barked sharply and nearly jumped away.

"Are we there?" asked Pete, staring into the fog.

"Yep. About ten feet away is the Kilpatrick River." He pressed his hand on the horn again.

"Why—why are you honking?"

Jackstraw climbed out and stood impatiently tapping his fingers on the hood. "Ferry must be on the other side. But that's odd. He hasn't much business this time of year, and from the looks of the road in, we're the first over it in days."

"How can the captain ever see to get back across?" Pete asked nervously. He was standing on the edge of the bank and could see nothing more than swift, deep-looking water swirling out and away from him. He put Crackers down on the grass. She bounded off and began to snuffle along the bank, where she immediately frightened a frog that leaped up under her nose and splashed into the river. Then Jackstraw began growling, and Pete knew something was wrong before he even looked up.

"Of all the rotten luck," fumed Jackstraw. He had walked out on the ferry's loading ramp and was reading some sort of notice posted on one of the abutments. Obviously it had given him only the worst of news.

"What's the matter?" Pete asked uneasily.

"The man who runs the ferry has gone to Victoria for a week."

Pete closed his eyes. Everything was against them!

Jackstraw came back and leaned against the truck, looking fierce, and mad, and just a little discouraged. "What a time to go on holiday," he said bitterly.

CHAPTER 10

Marooned

Pete flung himself down on the truck seat, completely crestfallen.

"Oh, there's another way across the river," Jackstraw said sourly. "So don't look so all fired glum."

"There is!"

"But like everything else in this day's march, it has its bad points." He backed the truck around with a roar, and they started up a rutted offshoot path that rocked them violently from one side to another. Carefully they crossed a small, deep gulley, forded a muddy backwater, and stopped. "Well, let's hope this ferry is in."

Pete squinted to see through the mists. "There's an old barge," he said, getting out and walking to the river. "But there isn't a ferry."

"I've news for you, boy," said Jackstraw, maneuvering the truck within inches of the bank. "That old barge *is* the ferry."

Pete's mouth dropped open, and he stared at the craft again. "Surely, that isn't it," he said, as Jackstraw began to check the wire cables that were strung from the barge to a rickety-looking tower set back in the trees. The wires were rusty, and they went through pulleys on the boat that looked even worse. "It doesn't look very safe," Pete said.

Jackstraw jumped to the barge, ignoring him. Crackers tried to make the leap to the deck and follow, but the distance was too great, and she fell in the water with a splash. She straggled out and ran cheerfully to Pete before she shook herself fiercely.

"You're a mutt," said Pete, and jumped away from her, then hopped out to the barge with Jackstraw.

The river was brown and muddy, not at all like the rushing Little Qualicum Creek they had forded. "Is it deep?" he asked Jackstraw.

"Yes. Not only that, it seems to be flooding, too. Be just as well to get across as soon as possible."

Pete examined the boat carefully. It was nothing more than a blunt-bowed barge, perhaps twelve feet wide and about twenty-five feet long, not a lot longer than the truck. It was made of wood and looked as old as Noah's ark. It had no rails at all; the only protection from walking off the edge was a small cap of about an inch. At each end and on the same side of the barge were two posts, as big around as himself and about waist-high, and in the top of each was a large pulley. The rusty cable stretched from the tower on the bank, through one sheave then through the other sheave and disappeared into the fog. Apparently the other end was attached to a similar tower on the opposite bank.

"How wide is this river anyway?" asked Pete.

"About seventy-five yards." Jackstraw threw off two lines holding the barge against a makeshift pier and gave the cable a pull. The vessel moved in to the bank with a bump. Somewhere on the splintery deck he found two narrow planks that he fitted over the bow and onto the grass.

"Are you going to drive aboard on those?"

Jackstraw nodded. "You'll have to see that I'm centered. Tilly's got such a short wheelbase, I need to get both back and front wheels on each plank just right." He climbed in the truck and attempted to adjust it into place, backing and then rebacking according to Pete's directions.

The work was not the least bit easy. The mud was as slippery as ice, and the barge bounced up and down irritably. Each time Pete got the boards placed, the barge moved slightly, and they juggled to one side. He began to perspire. Jackstraw was being very patient, following his instructions as well as he could.

At last both the front wheels were lined up, and Pete motioned with his fingers. "Come ahead slowly." The truck revved and began to crawl up the planks. Mud squeezed from the heavy treads and bits of leaves and sticks clung to the wood, making it difficult to see whether the truck was perfectly centered.

The climb was a steep few feet, but once all four wheels were on Jackstraw drove up easily, and the truck bounced onto the deck.

"There's not much room on this thing," Pete mused as he climbed aboard. "Are you sure all this weight won't sink it?"

"Never has yet. This was the only ferry across the Kilpatrick for years. Just got the new one about six months ago. Kept this ferry for emergencies, and I consider this just that. Well, grab the brainless beast, and let's go." Pete groaned and ran to pull Crackers out from under a rotten log. She had been digging and looked like a mud pie.

As soon as they were aboard, Jackstraw cast off the lines. "Don't you think you ought to start the motor first?" Pete asked. He didn't much like the looks of the river boiling around the hull.

"Engine? What engine?" said Jackstraw. "We just walk the thing across by pulling in on this cable."

Pete stared. Jackstraw was taking long-armed reaches along the cable and pulling the boat through the water. Quickly Pete lent a hand. "Why," said Pete, "it isn't hard at all. Even the current doesn't bother much."

"This ferry was in operation for nearly thirty years," Jackstraw explained. "It's not what I'd call newfangled and all that, but it usually works pretty well. Except for the dirt, that is."

Pete looked at their hands. They were a filthy brown from the rust and grease of the cable.

"Better tie up that dog," Jackstraw said, with a nod at Crackers. Pete gasped. She was hunched in an all-too-familiar stance ready to jump in the water. He caught her harness hastily.

"What your brother sees in that animal is beyond me," Jackstraw said with a grin.

Pete made a face and wondered himself. She was coated with mud, but unbearably lively and happy. The frayed cord was still on her collar, and Pete tied it to the truck bumper and went back to help Jackstraw.

"She pulls easily enough," the man said. "There's no need to help."

Pete stared out at the river, though he could not see much of it. "I wish this old fog would lift," he said.

"It's due to clear any time," announced Jackstraw. "Another hour or so."

"Say, what's that?" asked Pete, squinting his eyes as something loomed large and ominous upstream ahead of them. "Have we come to the other side already?"

Jackstraw peered ahead. "Shouldn't be yet. Oh-oh!" He brought the barge to a halt.

"It's only a tree," said Pete lightly, for now it was closer, and he could see it more clearly. Jackstraw quickly shoved the loading planks under the truck's wheels as blocks. "Whatever is the matter?" Pete asked startled, for Jackstraw's face was set in a frown. Pete looked back at the tree. There were bubbles of whitecaps and rapids as water swirled around and through the limbs.

"The water sure is high on this side," said he.

"That tree happens to be floating," Jackstraw said sharply. "It must have been toppled off the bank during the rise in water."

"Floating!" exclaimed Pete.

"And unless I'm mistaken, it's going to get tangled with our lead cable, and we're apt to get a good jolt."

Pete licked his lips. The sight of that great weight surging down on them was suddenly frightening. It was so near now he could see tiny, muddy whirlpools around the submerged parts. "It's going to hit us!" Pete cried.

"Now, let's think of something better than that. Look! The current's swinging it. Quickly! Lend a hand! Perhaps we can shoot on past."

Pete lunged for the cable. Between them the old barge moved faster than ever before. Crackers barked excitedly and tugged at her lead ready to leap out at the approaching giant. A strange, fluky swirl of water turned the tree almost completely around, and they could see the fresh, green color of the fluttering limbs. It looked like one of the tall, splintery-thin pines that grew so thickly in the North. There was another wild boil of water, and now the tree obviously was going to miss the barge and pass astern.

"We've cleared it!" Pete shouted in relief. "It's going on past!"

"Well, just you keep right on pulling there, boy," said Jackstraw. The sweat was standing out on his forehead, and his damp moustache clung to his cheeks.

Suddenly the barge lurched wildly. Pete fell to his knees, and Jackstraw swayed hard against the cable. The boat tipped precariously, and the truck rocked on the ancient floorboards with a squeak of springs. Again the barge shook; the whole boat heeled upstream, and water lapped over the rail.

"What happened?" cried Pete.

"Quickly!" said Jackstraw. "Lend another hand." Pete took his place at the cable and pulled. But there was no easy response from the barge. They jerked, then pulled again, but with no avail. The tree had caught in the cable behind them.

Jackstraw wiped his hand over his forehead, as they stared at the downed pine. It had twined and retwined itself into the wire and, in so doing, brought them to a complete stop. Wavelets and rapids had turned foamy-white as the current shot by its limbs and branches.

"Now that's a fine how-de-do," Jackstraw said, his hands hooked on his hips in disgust.

"We can't go either way," said Pete hollowly.

"You can see why they needed a new ferry, eh? This one sometimes does have its little problems."

"We're stuck," moaned Pete, and sat down on the truck step. Crackers leaped in his lap coating him with mud, but he didn't even care. "Boy, but are we stuck this time!"

CHAPTER 11

Over the River

"Now, now," soothed Jackstraw. "You are the most easily discouraged young man I've seen in a long time. In the spring this old bucket used to get stuck in mid-river nearly once a week."

Pete perked up slightly. "But how do we get the ferry into shore?"

Jackstraw sat down on the truck fender. "Well, the tree could break loose itself in a few minutes without anyone doing anything."

"And if it doesn't?" questioned Pete.

Jackstraw glanced at him with a sparkle in his eyes. "Then the ferry stays here until the man who runs it gets back from Victoria. He can take his punt out and chop the tree free."

"But that will be a whole week," Pete said in dismay.

"Then again, the constable and his deputies would most probably see us stranded, once the fog lifts and they arrive at the dock across the river. They would come get us in the speed launch." Jackstraw smoothed his moustache with his fingers and watched the hulking pine as it clung stubbornly around the cables astern.

"Might the weight of the tree even break the cable?" Pete asked fretfully.

"Could," admitted Jackstraw. He got up and began to rattle through the camp box. Pete followed him closely, but the man only was putting together methodically a ham-and-cheese sandwich. Pete hadn't the slightest appetite, and he waited nervously beside the truck for something to happen.

"If the wire should go," he said "wouldn't it be awfully dangerous for us?"

Jackstraw sat beside him and unscrewed the cap of the canteen. "Won't hurt a thing if it does break," he said lightly. "We would just go aground in the shallows." Pete guessed he must have looked frightened and that Jackstraw was trying to be reassuring. Crackers pressed her nose against Jackstraw's arm, and he handed her a taste of cheese, which she gulped down in a swallow. "Lots of times logs get caught," he went on. "If they are close to the barge, you can usually pry them away, though I'm afraid this one is just a little too far out."

He downed the last of his sandwich and drank long

from the water jug. In a few minutes he got up, walked to the stern of the boat, and began to joggle and shake the cable again. The pressure of the tree had forced it to sag underwater and far downstream, and moving the heavy wire the slightest bit was impossible. He looked at his watch.

"It's going to be dark soon," said Pete tightly. "Will we have to spend the night here?"

"Not if I can help it," Jackstraw said shortly. He tugged at his moustache irritably. "Blast and double blast," he said to the offending tree. "Why don't you move out?"

They sat for another hour, uncomfortable and impatient and beginning to get a little cold. The breeze had begun to pick up decidedly.

"Only good thing that's happened all day," said Jackstraw finally. "This wind is blowing away the fog. Look. You can see shore."

Pete looked up eagerly. Sure enough, he could make out the hazy riverbank from which they had come. In a few more minutes he could see the dim shape of the opposite side.

"It looks a long way off," he said unhappily.

"Not so very far."

Swirls of fog blew through the trees, and even as they watched it broke and thinned. Within minutes the world around them took on shape.

"Look at that!" said Pete, at his first glimpse of the precipitous peaks.

Wisps of clouds still clung spottily to the mountainsides like smoke. A waterfall, in the far, high distance, fell in jerky zigzags, and there was a giltlike glow all around as the sun tried, and then tried again, to shine through. Fireweed caught its first rays and burst into a purple-red blaze. White daisies along the shoreline looked starchy bright, and their yellow centers flashed across the expanse of water like dots of gold.

"What say we leave this lovely craft?" announced Jackstraw.

"Gladly," Pete answered drearily. "But if you think I'm going to swim for it you're crazy."

"Swim!" exclaimed Jackstraw. "What a nasty thought. I was thinking about climbing off on the cable."

Pete looked at the wire that stretched enticingly out over the water to the bank. "I'm not exactly a monkey," he said with a chuckle, as Jackstraw began to sort through the equipment in the truck. "Hey," he said quickly. "You were kidding, weren't you?"

"No, it's not awfully far," Jackstraw replied, handing him a back pack of gear he had gathered. "It isn't the best way ashore, but I can't see staying out here till we rot."

"You mean climb out on that skinny wire hand over hand?" said Pete, dumbfounded.

"Sure. You can wrap your legs around it and hold yourself up. Try it on that section of cable between the posts on deck there. It's not going to be a very clean way to get to the beach, but we can make it without much problem."

Pete raised his eyebrows slightly. He used to crawl along a pipe fence in faraway Seattle, but only for laughs. He gripped the wire with his hands, then swung his legs over the cable to support most of his weight. Although he hung down like a trussed bird, it wasn't as hard as he had thought to squirm his way along the wire. He got back to his feet and brushed his hands on his trousers.

"Think you can make it?"

Pete nodded. "But what about Crackers?"

Jackstraw emptied a small net bag that was holding some cans of motor oil and held it up. "We can put her in this, and I'll carry her."

Pete looked at the bag thoughtfully and at the wiggling Crackers.

"Oh, I won't drop her in the water intentionally," Jackstraw said slyly.

"Well, I guess I can make it," Pete answered. "I almost wish it was foggy again, and I wouldn't have to look at all that water. It looks ugly."

Jackstraw brought out a coil of line and tied an end around Pete, looped it up over his shoulder, and caught it at his waist again. Next he tied the opposite end around himself. He strapped on a heavy belt, which included a loop of rings and spikes and a sharp pick hammer. Pete couldn't stand it any longer. "What are all those things for?"

Jackstraw slung the extra coil of line over his shoulder and put on another pack. "For climbing Shadow Mountain." He rechecked Pete's lines, and then began to untie Crackers.

"You mean mountain climbing?"

Jackstraw picked up the little dog, and she lashed his face lovingly with her tongue. "Well, it is a mountain."

"But—but—"

"Shove that bag over her legs," Jackstraw ordered, as he wrapped his huge hands around the squirming dog to clamp her still. "What a worm."

Pete shoved in her tail and back legs, but they quickly popped through the thick mesh when she slid to the bottom. Jackstraw stuffed her front legs and head inside, closed the drawstring with a yank, and tied her to his belt. She flopped down like a captured pig.

"Do you really mean you have to climb Shadow Mountain like a mountaineer, and not just hike up it?"

"Parts. There was a trail, but we Indians managed to mess it up proper right. We undermined the path that was there and now have to go through a miserable climb if we want to get back up.

"Our ancestors used the mountain as a burial ground, a stepping-off spot for the great beyond, and we hated all those people up there tramping about, destroying shrines we hold sacred. And they always dig in that fool Shadow Mine. All we want is to keep outsiders away, the ones that simply aren't interested in anything but money. Considering it never had much silver that mine sure has a reputation. It draws men like honey draws bears."

"But when you blew up the path, didn't it keep the Indians away as well as the outsiders?"

"Well, now I personally didn't destroy it, you understand. Because, you see, I'm always the one who has to go up there and rescue the simpletons who try to climb it and get stuck."

"But don't the Indians use the burial ground anymore?"

Jackstraw shook his head. "No, but my people don't want intruders there. And just the idea of a cache makes some men do most anything. Like those two birds, Jasper and Benny. I'll bet no one alive could tell them there is no minable silver in Shadow Mine."

"Do you think they will hurt Dave?" Pete asked shakily.

"I doubt it. The worst they would probably do is leave him up there. If that happens and he starts down, he might have trouble. It would be easy to fall on the steeper parts. Dave could make it without any problem, though, if someone showed him the way."

"I've never mountain-climbed before," admitted Pete softly.

"Hmm. It will be easy enough. I can always haul you up in a bag like Crackers."

"A bag!" said Pete indignantly. "You won't put me in a bag!"

Jackstraw threw back his head and laughed loudly.

"You won't," said Pete angrily. "I'm not any old dog."

The man chuckled. "Well, all right, but now let's get across this river. I'll go first, and I want you to wait until I get out a ways before you start. If you don't, the weight of both of us on the cable close together might pull it down, and we'll be dragging in the water." And with that not very cheerful observation he swung his legs over the cable and hand over hand started working his way toward shore.

Pete hated to admit it, even to himself, but he was terrified. He waited nervously until Jackstraw shouted to him, then anxiously swung himself into position.

There were some things, Pete knew, that must be done despite his fear. And if he did not crawl across the wire, he never would be able to face Jackstraw again. The man might be only a guide, and not even one very famous or exceptionally wise, but he was facing a dangerous situation to help Dave. He would know Pete Fleming was a coward, and that thought was worse for Pete to bear than climbing out over the raging river on the sagging, dancing wire.

Once he started, he was startled to find his back was nearly dipping in the river. For a moment he almost went back to the safety of the stranded barge; in fact, he must have hesitated quite a long time, for Jackstraw shouted again, and the line around his waist took up with a snap. He arched his neck back and, upside down, saw Jackstraw far out ahead motioning to him impatiently.

Creeping along the wire was something like imitating an inchworm. It was reach, pull, reach, pull. In a matter of minutes his hands became inky-black with dirt and grease and dreadfully sore from the occasional sharp strands of wire that stuck out to snag his palms. The backs of his knees began to hurt, and his shoulders tired.

Then unexpectedly the barge surged heavily to one side, and the cable jerked and shook. Pete stopped crawling and hung on, desperately trying to keep from being thrown off. The wire swayed and danced and swung him high into the air. The next moment it came down, and he was dipped briefly into the river. The water was like ice, and it ran coldly down his back as he surged upward again.

"Hang on!" Jackstraw shouted. "The tree must be moving."

He was hanging on! But with each twang of the cable, he plunged lower and lower into the water. Pete felt the pull of the river as the current tried to pluck him away. He tasted the muddiness of the water, and when he rose up his matted hair fell wetly across his eyes, blinding him.

But as suddenly as the joggling had begun, it stopped. Pete held on motionless, clamped like a limpet to the thin strand, his heart pounding. The line around his waist tightened, but he was frozen in place.

"Hey, boy," shouted Jackstraw, and gave the line another pull. "Let's not spend the afternoon here!"

Pete unclenched his teeth and shook the hair from his eyes. The barge was still caught; the tree must have shifted only, for it was still stuck fast. Jackstraw gave the rope around his waist another tug, and reluctantly Pete began to move. By now he was over halfway to shore, and he tried to hurry, though his hands were so sore he could hardly close them.

Then Jackstraw began to whistle. It seemed an awfully peculiar time to burst into a tune. Then Crackers barked. Pete arched back his neck and saw that Jackstraw had reached the riverbank and swung to the grass. His heart lifted, and his spirits rose completely.

Then it happened. Once more the snagged tree moved. The wire tightened, bounced up, and Pete lost his handhold. The next moment he was dipped deeply into the water, and he flailed frantically to find the cable. In an instant he surged upward, out of the water hanging only by the clamp of his knees. He might just as well have been riding a wild bronco upside down. The cable gave another lurch, and he was dropped back into the water. Up again, and this time he was kicked off. He went flying into the air and down with an ungraceful splash.

Pete surfaced swimming, and almost immediately the line around his waist took up with a yank, and he was pulled underwater again. The next time up he was coughing and spitting water and found himself floundering in the marshy grass and weeds that lined the shore.

He found his footing and half standing, half swimming got to the bank. Then Crackers bounded out of the brush and began to bark joyously. In a moment Jackstraw appeared and smiled broadly, Pete's lifeline held in his hands.

"Looks as if I've caught myself a fair-sized trout," he said, as he pulled Pete to the grass.

"I s-sure c-can't say much for your ferry service," Pete said shakily.

Jackstraw helped him to his feet, and only then untied the line around their waists. "Should have put you in the bag, too," he said slyly.

Pete glared at him, but then couldn't help himself and laughed.

Jackstraw grinned. "You see, it wasn't so bad."

"Oh, sure, it was great," Pete answered, and pushed Crackers to one side. She hadn't suffered any apparent lessening of enthusiasm by her trip. She was not even damp. Neither was Jackstraw.

"And how come I'm the only one who got all wet?" he said grumpily, and dumped a stream of water from his boots.

CHAPTER 12

Base Camp

"I surely am getting sick of being half drowned all the time," Pete said gloomily, as he followed Jackstraw up a grassy path.

"If you can make it about a quarter mile, you can dry out for the night. It will be dark by then, and it's there we meet the constable."

"Will that be at the cliffs you were talking about?"

"That's right. You can see them in a bit. The first leg of Shadow Mountain."

They began to climb steeply, and the terrain switched from thick timber and brush to a section of barren earth covered with loose bits of black slate. Pete had trouble keeping his footing, and he struggled along, slipping and sliding. But Jackstraw had even more problems. Since he was heavier, his feet sank deeply in the rocky chips, and occasionally he was forced to use his hands for support. Small landslides slithered

away downhill behind them. Crackers was having no
trouble. She trotted over it all with tail flying.

"Blasted stuff," complained Jackstraw, as he turned
to give Pete a hand up onto solid ground again. "Makes
you go backward fast as you go ahead."

Pete panted heavily. "We sure are going straight
up," he gasped. "Are those the cliffs?" Jackstraw
glanced at the hulking slab of rock rising through the
tall trees, and nodded. "Is that what we have to climb?"
Pete exclaimed.

"Not tonight."

Pete plodded on thoughtfully. That sheer face ahead
looked as slick as glass and miles high. They crossed a
field of small white daisies pressed flat against the
grass. He was winded, but was doing everything in his
power to keep Jackstraw from noticing. Apparently he
wasn't putting on a very good show, because the man
stopped and waited for him to catch up.

"Bear up, boy," he said pleasantly. "You're almost
there."

Pete readjusted his wet pack and kept on. It was so
long since he had felt comfortable he nearly had forgotten what it was like. Yet he had left Pine Island
this morning. As they started across more loose shale,
he slipped and fell to his knees. Crackers ran up and
wiped his ear wetly with her tongue.

"Go away," he grumbled, and got unsteadily to his
feet. Immediately he slid backward helplessly. Then
Crackers jumped on his knees playfully, making him

lose his balance, and he tumbled over. "Yikes!" he screeched, as he came to a grinding halt flat on his back. Crackers licked him on the cheek and shoved her cold nose into his neck. "Ooo! You coyote," he moaned.

"What are you doing playing with the dog?" Jackstraw called back to him. "Let's get to the cabin."

Pete staggered on up the incline. "I'm *not* playing," he mumbled, trying to shake Crackers away from his cuff. "Did you say a cabin?"

"Right there."

"Oh!" Pete looked up eagerly. "Oh, it really is!" He slipped again and went down on his knees. Crackers leaped for his wrist, and then chewed at his sweater button.

"And it looks as if the constable is already there," Jackstraw went on absently.

Pete shook Crackers free and crept up beside him. There was a trickle of smoke coming from the chimney.

"But I can't understand how he got here ahead of us," the man added thoughtfully. "With the river flooding it would be a mean job getting here, and," he went on grimly, "I didn't see that speed launch he was to use tied up along the riverbank."

"A fire," whispered Pete. "That will really feel neat."

Crackers began to chew the heel of Jackstraw's boot, and he glanced at her impatiently. "Dog, why don't you go chase squirrels?" He kicked her aside, but Crackers only charged back with a playful growl.

"Oh, do stop playing with the dog," commanded Pete solemnly, wiping the perspiration from his forehead.

Jackstraw grinned and gave Pete a pull out of the stones to a path with firmer footing.

As they came closer, Pete saw that the cabin was very tiny. It was made of logs, roughly put together, and had a sod roof. There was a stone fireplace on one side and a door, which was open. As they approached, a man came out and held up his hand in greeting. He was short and rather heavy, and he wore a sweater that could have been a twin to Pete's. Obviously he was an Indian, and Jackstraw seemed to know him quite well. They grinned and shouted at each other pleasantly.

Crackers dashed ahead and leaped affectionately at the stranger. He patted her warmly, then began to talk seriously to Jackstraw. Pete listened for a minute, but as they were speaking Indian he understood nothing, so he went inside the cabin.

The room was warm and smelled of smoke. It was also very dark, the only light flickering from the fire-place and the last glow of daylight coming from the open doorway. Pete threw down his pack and held out his hands to the fire. A large cross section of a tree served as a table of sorts, and beside the fire was a stack of wood. There wasn't much else in the room, not even a window. Well, there were mosquitoes. He swatted one biting his wrist just as Jackstraw came inside with the man.

"This is Elmer Fishcatcher," he introduced him.

"How do you do?" said Pete politely. "I'm awfully worried about my brother. Do you think he's all right?"

Jackstraw sighed and then translated. In a moment he turned back to Pete. "Elmer isn't the constable, Pete. In fact, he's brought some rather bad news."

Pete's hands tightened into fists.

"Constable Perry can't get up the Kilpatrick River because of high water." He hesitated for a moment. "It seems he came up the sixty miles on Chikamin Sound without any problem, but once at the mouth of the Kilpatrick he was faced with the flood current and couldn't make the last leg. I was afraid of that when I didn't see the speedboat." He stroked his red moustache absently.

"He's gone back down the sound to Indian Camp, and I'm to go there and meet him. That way I can take him and his deputies overland along the same route we took and bring him back here to start up the mountain."

Elmer threw another log on the fire, and from somewhere in the depths of the darkness he brought out a worn blanket and handed it to Pete.

"Get off those wet clothes," Jackstraw ordered roughly. "And start drying out. I'll get tea brewing and something to eat."

Pete was glad the cabin was dark. He wouldn't have been able to stand having the men see his tears. Jackstraw rattled the cooking tins noisily and kneeled before the fire.

"But I can't go back," he said to Pete, as he rummaged through the packs looking for tea. "With Tilly stuck in mid-river, I'd have to walk all the way. I couldn't get them all back for at least two or three days over that ground we covered."

Pete wiped his eyes with the back of his hand and carefully spread out his wet clothes to dry.

"Any way you take it," Jackstraw went on, "it would be a long time before we could start up."

Pete huddled in front of the fire wrapped in the scratchy blanket and waited breathlessly for him to finish.

"So I'm going to go on up," Jackstraw blurted shortly.

"Oh!" Pete gasped. "Oh, yes!"

"I don't want to go up, you understand that. Without the constable, this might get awfully complicated."

"Will—will Mr. Fishcatcher go along?"

"No. His wife is in Bella Coola, and he has to take care of the children. There's five of them, and all very small. He could only leave them for a little while to tell me what happened to the constable."

"But how did he know?"

"He has a radio transmitter. Surely, by now you know most people that live in this country have to have contact with the outside. Elmer lives downriver a few miles." He dumped the canteen of water into a pan and put it on to heat. "I want you to stay with Elmer," he announced hurriedly. "You will have a place to sleep and enough to eat. It won't be very fancy, but Elmer is a good man."

"No!" gasped Pete, leaping to his feet. "Jackstraw, I'm going. You can't leave me behind now."

"I'm not leaving you. It's just that I can—I can—"

"Travel faster? Is that what you're trying to say? Well, have I held you up so far?" Pete demanded. "Have I?"

Jackstraw moved uneasily. "Pete," he said quietly, "it's just that I can face them up there better if I don't have to worry about you. I shouldn't have brought you in the first place, but I thought Perry and his deputies would be here."

"I'll do what you tell me. I always have. Even to creeping off that stupid ferry."

"It's not that."

"I'll keep out of sight. I'll never even open my mouth. I'll do everything you say!"

"Blast!"

"Please," begged Pete, his eyes swimming. "Please!"

"You don't understand," Jackstraw said, frowning. "You can't go because it—oh, double blast anyway!" He slammed his hand against the fireplace violently. Then he turned to Elmer Fishcatcher and growled an explanation. And Pete breathed again. For apparently he was telling the man that he would go with him to the summit.

The Indian nodded, then lowered his pack to the fire. Jackstraw went through the meager supply offered and set aside a few things to keep. Elmer packed up the remainder, and with a shake of Pete's hand, and then Jackstraw's, he wished them luck and good-bye. They watched from the doorway as he made his way slowly down the zigzag toward the river and finally out of sight.

"Thank you," whispered Peter.

"I must have rocks in my head," Jackstraw grumbled, and went back to preparing the meal. Pete emptied his wet pack on the floor and laid his things out to dry. Before long, they spooned up platefuls of steaming stew and cups of hot, strong tea.

Crackers wiggled up on her stomach, smacked her lips, and drooled hungrily.

Pete looked at her with concern. "We should have let Mr. Fishcatcher take care of her till we get back."

Jackstraw scraped a helping on the stone hearth for the dog, and she lapped it up noisily. "I asked him," he said. "But someone has put out poisoned bait for coyotes, and it's killed all his own dogs. He said he would take her if it was what we really wanted."

"Oh, no!" said Pete. "That would be awful."

Jackstraw nodded, and they went to the doorway for a last look before full dark. Pete studied the steep, precipitous cliff rising at their feet, its heights lost in purple, dark shadows. A faint call of a night bird sounded in the distance, lonely and rather sad.

"We're coming," Pete whispered. "Dave, we're coming."

CHAPTER 13

The Climb

Jackstraw was singing some singsong Indian chant. Pete opened his eyes, stretched, and sat up to face the morning. His every bone ached.

"I feel as if I'd been run over," he moaned.

"There's cereal in that pot," said Jackstraw. "Eat hearty. We can't stop till late."

Pete crawled to the fire and spooned the hot food into his tin cup. Then he sprinkled it liberally with sugar and ate. It did not taste very good.

"I've only included the necessities," Jackstraw went on. "Most of it's food and a change of clothes."

"I'll probably need those," said Pete dryly. "I'm forever getting wet."

"You told me yesterday you had never climbed before."

Pete finished eating and wiped out the cup and spoon with his towel. "That's right." He pulled on his pack.

120

"Ever scrambled?"

"Whatever's that?" He stood up and let Jackstraw put the end of one coil of line around his waist.

"Oh, you know. Going up steep places. Where you might have to use your hands a lot."

Pete held up his arms until the knot was tied, then examined it closely. "Well, yes, I guess I've done that."

"Do you mind heights?"

Pete shook his head, jerked at the line, and decided it was very secure. Jackstraw neatly coiled the rest of the rope and showed him how to put it over his head, with one arm through. It lay against his side quite comfortably.

As they left the cabin, the cliff above them looked shining silver, as the sun, just up, was reflected in the drizzle of water that seeped down its face. They followed a game trail along the foot of the mountain, and Pete fell into step beside Jackstraw. "Are we going to go right up that wall?" he asked a little uneasily.

"Good grief, no," answered Jackstraw, looking up. "We'd need to be human flies to get up there. We go down about a quarter mile to the main trail."

"But I thought you said it had been destroyed?"

"It has, but farther up. We've a steep hike yet."

Crackers dashed in and out of sight along the edge of the path. Her nose pressed to the ground as she searched eagerly for some sign of life to chase.

"Jackstraw," Pete said finally, "I've been wondering about those awful men holding Dave prisoner. Do you

think there might be more silver in the mine than anyone suspects, and only Jasper and Benny know about
it?"

"I can't see how. The tribe had some mining engineers up from Victoria some years ago to make sure."

"Is the mine very large?" Pete asked.

"No, just a couple of tunnels off one main shaft. The
only thing I can think," Jackstraw went on thoughtfully, "is perhaps they believe there may be some other
material in the mine."

"You mean diamonds or something like that?" Pete
asked excitedly.

"Hardly diamonds."

"Then what?"

"I don't know. Did they mention anything about
some other metal?"

Pete thought back. "No. They only talked about the
silver." He sighed. "Well, actually, they didn't talk
about silver either. It was Dave who did that."

"What about equipment? What did they have?"

Pete struggled to recall. "They took Dave's pick and
shovel. There was a line tent, and some food, and camp-
ing gear."

"Maps or charts?"

Pete shook his head. "The one called Benny had a
big camera he brought to the cabin. He had it strapped
across his shoulder. I guess all their stuff was in the
plane. I never got a look inside it."

"No doubt. Did he use the camera at all?"

"No. In fact, the more I think of it, the more I'm not sure it was a camera. Perhaps it was a radio. It was sort of strange-looking and had lots of wires and junk."

Jackstraw came to a halt. The path ahead began to wind through some huge boulders that towered over their heads. They looked as if at one time they had rolled off the top of the mountain. "We'll go single file from here on," he said. "Now follow close behind, but if you get tired, speak up, and we can stop for a breather."

"What about Crackers?"

"She's all right. If she falls off the edge, it will be her own funeral. But surely even she has enough sense to stay on the path. Ready?"

Pete nodded, and they started through the massive rocks. Crackers was already out of sight ahead, and her bark echoed back to them hollowly.

"Will they hear her?" Pete asked, thinking of Jasper and Benny.

"No. We're a long way from the top. But we'll have to muzzle her when we get nearer. Can't have her roaring like a lion when we get up there."

In a few minutes they came out of the giant boulders. Pete saw they had climbed partially above the base of the cliff, and he touched the cold slickness of its face. Then his interest was taken by a narrow path on the sheer wall. Some fluky upheaval of earth conveniently had left a climbing shelf of jutting rock, as neatly formed as any man-made path.

Jackstraw hesitated before starting up. "I'll rope us," he said. "This gets pretty steep in a bit." He took the looped end of Pete's line and tied it around himself. "I'm giving us about eighty feet." He coiled a length of the rope, held it in his hand, and showed Pete how to hold it. "The object of this loop is for you to let it out, or take it in, without jerking me backward. It works the other way, too. Saves yourself from getting pulled forward if I go too fast.

"Now keep this safety line around you placed high." He gave the rope a jerk up to Pete's armpits. "And, boy, there's an old flatlanders' saying about not looking down from a height or you'll get scared. I'm not for that. Look back all you want. If you don't mind heights, you won't be much bothered. It's just like going up in an elevator." And with those instructions he set off. Pete let the line run out between them, then followed before it took up, and held it loosely without letting it drag on the ground.

The shelf was about four feet wide, very steep, and covered with bits of dirt and small clumps of grass, which clung to it stubbornly. The face was fissured with cracks, and in some of them more growth appeared. Here and there a few dwarfed and twisted scrub, their roots exposed, hungrily twined across the rocks.

Gradually Pete got used to the altitude. The world began to spread out below him. At first, all he could see were the thick pines, but then the Kilpatrick River appeared, and Jackstraw pointed out the stranded ferry.

Tilly still was marooned, for the clinging, obstinate tree remained fast to the cables. Beyond the river was the ridge they had skated down in the mud, and later Chikamin Sound hove up before him.

"That's pretty," said Pete. Far, far to the west, in the purple haze of distance, was the Pacific.

Now the path was getting narrower, the drop below them taking on more disturbing proportions. Those giant boulders had become the size of tiny stones. The grass underfoot disappeared, and loose bits of dirt and gravel made the footing slippery and unsure. The way ahead seemed to be leading straight into a giant crack in the cliff.

As they came up to it, Jackstraw halted. Crackers was lying in the shade of an overhanging rock and jumped up to meet them. A small trickle of spring water fell from the heights, and through the years a tiny pool had formed in the stone. Ferns and grass and tiny yellow flowers hugged the rock, and a bird skittered out of the deeper crevice and banked off into space.

Pete licked his lips. Their way was barred now, for what had been the trail to the opposite side of the fissure was gone. It simply had disappeared. The drop off the edge was frightening, and Pete stepped back beside the tiny pool and sat down. Jackstraw was scooping water into his hand, drinking.

"That's a long step," Pete said carefully.

Jackstraw wiped his wrist across his mouth. "Sure is. Now here's the deal. I'm going over, and I'll set the pitons in a very unsporting way, but today we aren't out to prove what sort of climbers we are. Once I'm on the other side, I'll tell you how to follow up."

From his belt he took one of the metal spikes and using the hammer drove it into the rock beside the pool. The metallic ping echoed crisply in the still morning air. When it was placed, he snapped on a ring, and then secured Pete's line through it and back to himself. "Now sit tight," he said, "and I'll give you a rest stop for a bit."

Pete settled himself in the shade and let Crackers climb into his lap. Jackstraw readjusted his belt, the coil of line around his shoulder, and began to inch his way along the split rock. It looked dangerous and completely unsafe. When he was dangling precariously over space he reached out with his fingertips, caught hold of a splinter-thin ledge, and hung on. Then he slithered his boot along another minute-sized crack until he was even farther away from the security of the path. The climbing went on for a few minutes until Pete found he was sitting so tensely his whole body ached. He could see a larger ledge Jackstraw was trying to reach, and though it was only about four feet away, the distance seemed like miles at the rate he was moving.

The minutes ticked by, while Pete's eyes remained glued to Jackstraw. The man used his hands as if the rock were something alive and not very trustworthy. He felt each slick face, each crack and fissure, very gently and cautiously. Another five minutes, another few

inches. Crackers wiggled in his arms and woofed, turning Jackstraw's attention back to them. Pete clamped the dog still. The bird, carrying something in her beak, flew back with a flurry of wings and disappeared inside the crevice. Jackstraw moved slowly ahead.

Pete stirred uneasily. He never would be able to do that. Never ever would he be able to climb out there. He would fall straight off that dinky ledge down to the bottom of the cliff.

Now Jackstraw was holding to the sheer wall with the fingers of one hand and pounding in a piton with the other. It was very difficult to do, for he hadn't enough room for a good swing. Pete pressed his lips together when the hammer slipped once, but the spike had been set. Jackstraw snapped on a ring, and through it strung a rope, which he promptly proceeded to yank and jerk violently about, making sure the piton was holding properly. Without a moment to relax, he began to work his foot out for the next step.

The ledge had become a tiny bit wider now, and Jackstraw's handholds seemed to be better spaced. On occasion, he used the pick hammer to chew out a better grip. But always he was setting the pitons. After a bit he looked threaded to the cliff, like a spider spinning its web. A half hour passed before, at last, he swung himself onto the main path opposite.

Pete got to his feet and let Crackers run free.

"Now—" said Jackstraw pointedly, as he coiled his line neatly and very carefully.

They weren't more than twenty feet apart, yet Pete felt he might as well have been a moon man gazing at faraway Earth. He fiddled with his own rope, nervously running it through his hands.

"I'll toss this end over," Jackstraw said quietly.

Pete dropped the line and caught the one flying at him.

"Hook those two packs to the snap on the end of the line I just sent you. Now tie the end of your rope on the packs." Pete did as he was told and looked up. "All right." Jackstraw nodded. "Take that mesh bag we use for Crackers out of my pack and keep it, then send the packs off over the ledge. Keep your end snug, so the gear won't beat against the rock."

"Ferry service, deluxe," said Pete, as the bags slipped over the expanse of space. Jackstraw pulled them up to his feet, untied the lines, and tossed them back again.

"Now, lucky you," Jackstraw said, smiling. "All by yourself you get to stuff that dog in the sack."

Pete gasped. "You mean we'll ferry her over, too?"

"That's right."

Pete picked up the bag and called Crackers. She came happily enough, her tail wagging, and he clamped his hand on her harness and lifted her up. She wiggled and twisted and flapped her legs like a lobster. "Ooo! Keep still." Her feet and legs kept popping out of the mesh at unwanted angles. She licked his face, chewed his wrist, barked, and slobbered on his hand.

"Ooo!" Pete gasped, and looked helplessly across at

Jackstraw. He grinned and waved. Pete gritted his teeth, clamped the dog more tightly, bunched her in an undignified ball, and pushed her, tailfirst, in the bag with a rush. Quickly he closed the drawstring and breathed in relief. She promptly began to chew at the netting. "Stop that!" said Pete sharply, and picked her up.

"Tie it well," Jackstraw said. "That animal can't be trusted for an instant." Pete obliged. "Now hook my line and yours the same way as you did on the packs."

"All set," Pete said, and ran his tongue over his lips. "Gently."

Jackstraw began taking in his end, while Pete carefully let his out. Crackers slid along the path, then dropped off into space, bounced up and down a few times, and made her trip across the expanse. Jackstraw pulled her in, untied the lines, and let her out of the bag. She shook herself sharply, slipped and teetered on the very edge of the drop. Pete gasped. Jackstraw yanked her in nearer the wall. Then she was off, gaily bounding away up the path beyond.

Pete wiped his sweaty hands on his trousers. His turn had come now.

"I want you to pay close attention, boy," Jackstraw said clearly. "This won't be hard to do."

"I—I don't think I can make it," Pete confessed shakily, looking at the space separating them. "Jackstraw, I thought I could, but I can't. I just can't."

CHAPTER 14

Over the Top

Jackstraw held up his hand. "Be still, and listen. You aren't going to climb over here the way I did. You're coming over in a pendulum."

Pete stared at him blankly. "A what?"

"It's called a pendulum. I'll swing you across. Now I've rigged two lines, and I'll pass them over to you. Catch."

Pete sorted them out, then looked to see where they were attached on the face of the wall and back at Jackstraw.

"It's sort of a seat rappel," Jackstraw went on calmly. "Put the ropes between your legs, one line up on the outside of each thigh. Keep them straight. Now across your shoulders, and let them hang down out of the way."

Pete looked at the lines, carefully examined the way

they were put, then glanced back at the expanse he needed to cross.

"Send over the end of that rope I've secured next to the pool there." Pete tossed it over to him. "Now make sure you have the other end of this hooked over your shoulder, around, fastened." Pete checked and then double-checked.

"What—what do I do now?" Pete asked unsteadily.

"Just hang on, and enjoy the ride."

Pete cringed and backed against the safety of the cliff wall.

"Ready?" Jackstraw asked. "Just sit in those ropes as if it was a swing. Down, down. Put your weight on it. You don't have to hold the lines so tightly; they won't slip. Relax."

Pete stared across the chasm dumbly. Jackstraw was watching him with shuttered eyes, a look a man gives to a frightened child, and it wasn't one Pete liked.

"I'm scared," he admitted weakly.

Jackstraw grunted. "Do you think I'd let something happen to you?"

Pete shook his head.

"You'll be across inside ten seconds."

"What if something should break?" he asked.

Jackstraw sighed. "Then you'll hold me up. And it's your brother needs the help."

Pete moved away from the security of the pool and very cautiously sat in the ropes as if on a swing.

"Move to the ledge, Pete, and get your feet over.

Farther. I've got you. That's it. Now when you slide off entirely, there's going to be a jolt, and the lines are going to take up around your legs and give you a good squeeze."

Pete inched out. "N—now?" he asked.

"A little bit farther."

Pete worked closer to the edge of the path. Pebbles scraped under him and rolled off and away below. He leaned out and looked toward the base of the cliff.

"Off you go now," Jackstraw said patiently. The seconds ticked by, one after another. "Pete. Pete. Hey, let's get this show on the road."

He never should have looked down! It was a million, billion miles of reeling, whirling world beyond him. The perspiration popped out on his forehead. He felt sick and dizzy. Jackstraw's voice sounded far, far away.

"Just push off, boy," the man said gently.

There could be nothing worse than this moment. Nothing more terrifying. Pete leaned forward, his eyes tightly closed, hands clenched on the ropes like a pair of vises, and slipped over the edge. He lurched sharply and dropped with a bump. The next second he was slowly twirling through space, an airplane without wings. Jackstraw pulled him in, and in a moment he touched the opposite cliff face and was hoisted up and onto the path.

He lay on top of the packs, shaking like a leaf in the wind, while Jackstraw loosened the ropes, took off one, then another, rolling him around like a sack of meal.

"Time to move on, Pete, We've a ways to go."

He sat up groggily and let Jackstraw strap the pack on his back. He handed him his rope neatly coiled, helped him to his feet, and shoved his hat back on his head.

"If it's any consolation," Jackstraw said, as they started out, "that's the worst of the lot."

Pete knew he was a simple, useless coward. His legs felt like rubber, and he hugged the wall nervously. Yet, coward or not, he had crossed that ugly place. He had really and truly crossed it! He breathed more steadily, straightened up, and his step became firmer. He even managed a weak grin, and Jackstraw clapped him on the shoulder.

Around the next turn, the path widened unexpectedly, and they had grass underfoot once more. Pete was startled to see a lone, sentinel pine loom up ahead. Jackstraw took in rope and walked beside him.

"This goes for about a mile, then over that hogback ridge we'll narrow down again."

Pete touched the bark of the tree as they passed. It was a friendly feeling, and suddenly the climb seemed bearable once more. That precipitous drop took some getting used to, but now it did not seem quite so awful as it had farther back. Another pine appeared, and another. Like soldiers, stairstepping single file, they marched up the steep trail before them.

"Look!" exclaimed Jackstraw. "How do you like that for mountain climbing?"

Off to their right, on what appeared to be the slick, unmarred face of a cliff, was a white, long-haired goat.

"What's holding him on?" said Pete.

"There's another, and more up ahead."

The animals spurted away from the trail to the forbidding mountainside. No cautious inching forward for them. They ran, jumped, and leaped, clinging to ledges and cracks Pete couldn't even see.

"Don't I wish I could climb like that," he said wistfully.

Jackstraw chuckled. "You do all right. I'd rather have you along than most of the parties I get." He glanced at Pete. "At least, you do what you're told."

Pete felt a rush of pleasure at the sly compliment, and then Crackers barked.

"She's the cause of their fright," said Jackstraw. "It looks as if she's even managed to tree a few."

She certainly had. When they reached the twisted dwarf pine where Crackers stood guard, they could see two of the mountain goats balanced in the branches above her.

Jackstraw picked up the dog and held her squirming and barking under his arm. "If mama goat comes down that trail after you, dog, you just might end up in Madagascar."

They were babies, Pete could see, and their coats weren't as pretty and shiny as they had seemed in the distance. "They're cute," he said, prying the branches apart for a better look, as they bleated like lost lambs.

"Hmm. Well, an irritated mother may see you, and you'll end up in Madagascar, too. Come on. They aren't especially keen on the likes of us."

There was only one more really bad place for them to climb. Jackstraw had been right when he said they were over the worst of the pitch. After they crossed the ridge and started up the final half, the way got very narrow. When they reached one especially difficult ascent, Jackstraw stopped, placed a piton, and tied Pete onto it. The ledge they were on was no more than a foot wide, and Pete felt as if he was standing on the very edge of space.

"I feel like an eagle," he said, as Jackstraw left him to begin climbing up a chimneylike crack.

"Well, don't fly away."

Pete nodded and looked at Crackers once more in her mesh bag slung from Jackstraw's belt. She looked terribly uncomfortable, but resigned to her fate. Jackstraw worked into the narrow crevice and pushed himself up with the help of his feet and hands. The ledge he was heading for was a length away and straight up.

Pete put his back to the cliff face and looked out over the ever-widening view. Trees and meadows were every shade of green, while the creeks and lakes and sound were a turquoise blue. Somewhere out there, among the maze of islands in the ever-spreading Chikamin Sound, would be Pine Island. Usually about this time of day, Dave and he would be about to have their lunch. Coffee probably would be perking on the wood stove; perhaps a pie would be ready to come out of the oven. Pete sighed. He wondered if those two men would feed his brother.

Suddenly a line dropped on his head, and he looked up. Jackstraw was already standing on the ledge above. The rope was looped around his hips; the end he had sent down for Pete.

"I'm belayed up here, so get that line tied on you."

Slowly Pete knotted it as he had been showed.

Jackstraw gave it a few good jerks and looked at it carefully from above. "Okay. You're on your own now. You know what to do."

Carefully Pete untied his belay behind him, and then, using the piton as a handhold, slowly inched over and adjusted himself sideways in the crevicelike crack. He put his feet on its opposite wall, and by shoving and pushing with his feet, back, and hands, bit by bit he wormed his way up just as Jackstraw had done. The climb was not awfully difficult, and if he should slip he wouldn't have far to fall. Even if the line Jackstraw held should break, he could drop only the few feet back to the ledge. He ran his tongue over his lips. That is, if he stopped at the ledge and didn't tumble over beyond.

Pete felt the sweat begin to bead on his forehead. He stopped, glanced up, and Jackstraw winked at him. It was the reassurance he needed; he moved up the last of the way and slithered onto the ledge beside him.

"I don't think I'll ever like climbing mountains," said Pete.

Jackstraw grunted. Pete coiled his rope and put it

over his shoulder. When he bent to pick up his pack, he saw Crackers still stuffed in the bag. She squirmed and wiggled and chewed at the cord angrily. He knelt to let her out.

"No." Jackstraw put his hand on his arm. "I have to muzzle her."

"Then we're close?" Pete gasped.

"All the way up."

Pete stood up and glanced about.

"It's a ways to the mine yet," Jackstraw went on, "but to be on the safe side I want this beast kept quiet."

"Shouldn't we leave her in the bag?" Pete asked anxiously.

"If she doesn't behave herself. I don't expect she's going to like this, but it will keep her still."

Crackers was pawing and scratching, trying to tear away the leather strap that Jackstraw had put over her mouth. He also had tied a heavy line through her harness as a leash, one she couldn't possibly break.

"Will she pull off that thing on her face?" Pete asked.

"I don't think so. Are you ready? The trail up here has pretty well grown over, but I'm going to circle around just the same. Now go quietly. Foreign sounds are easily picked up."

Pete swallowed. Now that he had finally reached the top of Shadow Mountain, all he felt was a prickle of his skin, the prelude to that cold fear he had become so well acquainted with the past few days.

CHAPTER 15

Scratch One Helicopter

Jackstraw made no effort to choose the easiest route to Shadow Mountain Mine, and Pete fought to keep unstuck from some unpleasant, shoulder-high shrub covered with thorns. Nor could he move quietly unless he paid the closest attention. Jagged rocks and crags jutted up at unexpected places and broke underfoot with a rattle of falling stones. Crackers was on a lead so short her front feet barely touched the ground, and she became stubborn and uncooperative.

There was a small rise ahead, and they kept low as they crept to its crest. Pete's heart was pounding. Whatever were they going to do? Jasper and Benny both had guns. That antique relic of Jackstraw's, useless as it had been, still was strapped to the gun rack in the stranded truck. Little help it was to them now. Jackstraw looked cautiously over the ridge, then motioned to Pete.

Pines grew here and there, with thick brush covering the rest of the rough, uneven terrain. A wind whistled eerily and sent Pete's hair flying. He gasped and clutched Jackstraw's arm. In a tiny, minute-sized clearing was the helicopter.

"No one seems about," Jackstraw said, as he raised up slightly and scanned the area with sharp eyes.

"Where are they?" Pete asked.

"At the mine probably. It's over that next ridge." He sank down beside Pete again and took off his pack, then his belt holding the pitons and carabiners. Next he motioned to Pete to remove his own pack and shoved everything into the dense brush. The only things they had kept out were the climbing ropes and the hammer.

"The first thing," Jackstraw said softly, "is to disable that helicopter."

Pete blinked. "But they'll see us or hear us anyway."

"Possibly. But if they've set up camp at the mine, their interest will be there." He rolled up the collar of his jacket. "If we have any luck at all, this wind might even bring in the fog."

Pete shivered. It was dreadfully cold. The wind, the wisps of swiftly moving clouds just over the treetops, all added to the feeling of desolate loneliness. The helicopter took on all the appearance of an ugly, hulking, wire bug.

"I surely don't know much about helicopters," Jackstraw admitted. "Least of all, how to make one unflyable. But let's go see what can be done."

They inched down the slippery shale to a small animal trail, and from there skittered farther down the incline to the clearing. Carefully they moved from tree to tree, watching and listening for sign of life. But there was only the moaning wind. When they stopped the next time, they were beside the plane.

The helicopter was not very large, and Jackstraw made two complete circles around it before his interest centered at the stern, where he stood meditatively chewing his lip.

"Are you going to do something to that little propeller?" Pete whispered.

The man was feeling along the hub and the assorted gears around it. "This is the tail rotor," Jackstraw explained absently. "If this doesn't work, it can't get off the ground."

He went to the cabin and tried the door; it opened, and he looked inside. "Climb in, boy, and see what you can find." He gave Pete a hand up, then shut the door.

Pete swallowed. The glass was tinted a dusky green and made the cabin murky and dark. He opened two small lockers and quickly shuffled through papers and oily rags. Behind the front seat was a small box that held a few charts. Under the bench for the rear seat was an empty cardboard carton. The door opened, and Jackstraw pushed his head inside. "I've found some tools. Is there a radio in here?"

Pete nodded. The headphones were sitting on the seat. Just where the controls were located was a mystery.

The instrument panel was a mass of dials and switches and levers with silver handles.

"Come give me a hand," Jackstraw whispered.

Pete jumped out hastily. "Are you going to call for help on the radio?"

"Later. Right now let's get this thing inoperable."

Crackers was tied to one of the plane's landing skis, and she busily pawed her muzzled face. Jackstraw had found two wrenches, and Pete climbed inside the metal fuselage framework to hold one in place. It was dirty work; grease smeared his hands and got in his hair. Once the wrench slipped and hit the metal with a clink.

Pete gasped and looked at Jackstraw in panic.

"Try again," the man whispered with a hasty glance over his shoulder. "I have to get this backed off."

The job was ridiculously simple. In a matter of minutes they had completely removed the tail rotor. It was small and not even so awfully heavy.

"What are we going to do with it?" Pete asked, as they lowered it to the ground.

Jackstraw jerked his head toward a stand of pines. "That way."

Pete held one of the blades, Jackstraw the other, and they started off with it between them. "Crackers!" Pete whispered. "We forgot Crackers." Jackstraw gritted his teeth, dropped his end of the blade to the ground, and ran back. He untied the dog and pulled her after him. She was as balky as a little mule. They picked up the rotor again and half walked, half ran for the cover of

the trees. Up they went over a rise and dropped into a silty pit of pine needles.

Quickly Jackstraw ran his hands over the ground cover and gently began to move it aside. By the time the rotor was covered, Pete had to stare at the ground carefully to tell where it was buried.

Jackstraw sat back on his heels and dusted his hands. "They won't get off the mountain now," he said grimly, and then stood up. "Let's get to the mine." He looked at Pete carefully. "We must go very quietly, even though we do have the wind in our favor."

Pete nodded. "It's spooky up here," he said uneasily.

"That's my ancestors," Jackstraw said softly. Then he added with a wink, "Or so some say, anyway."

"Where—where is the burial ground?" Pete asked quietly.

"At the mine. It was years ago, during a burial ceremony, that they accidentally discovered the silver."

Pete swallowed. He could almost feel something weird and ghostly in the very air. They started out again, Crackers once more half off the ground as she hung from Jackstraw's firm hand. The clouds had become thicker and began to swirl through the tops of the trees. The wind thrashed the branches, and they wailed fearfully. Pete ran his hand through his hair. It was wet with the dampness of the coming fog.

In a few minutes Jackstraw put his lips to Pete's ear. "We are over the main tunnel now." He pushed Pete down to the ground and handed him Cracker's lead.

"Over this hump is a drop that is the face in which the entrance of the main shaft is located. Now sit tight till I have a look."

Crackers climbed into Pete's lap and smothered him with love. He adjusted her muzzle a little straighter and watched Jackstraw.

Yes, he was an Indian. Pete could tell that now, no matter his Irish mother and his red hair. It was apparent in the way he seemed to be a part of the rock on which he knelt, his eyes partly closed, his hair moving in the wind like the leaves of the scrub beside him. Pete shivered, suddenly ever so glad that Jackstraw was his friend.

In a moment the man slipped down beside him, and whispered. "Dave's there."

Pete felt the tears flood his eyes. "Is he all right?"

Jackstraw nodded. He put his finger to his lips and motioned Pete to look over the edge.

Dave! Pete wanted to call out, to make a signal and let him know they had come. He was sitting on a log covered with a sleeping bag. He wasn't tied and looked just as he had when Pete had last seen him. Jackstraw motioned for him to look directly below them. Pete sucked in his breath sharply and shrank lower. Not more than twenty feet away was Jasper. He didn't seem to have a gun, but he was the one who owned the pistol, so it might be in his pocket. At the moment he was leaning against a rock drinking what looked like a cup of coffee.

There was a small fire going beside Dave, and he seemed to be tending it. He glanced at it occasionally, once poking it into flames with a short stick. Then he went back to whatever held his attention. Pete blinked. Why, he was playing cards!

Jackstraw nudged him in the ribs, and Pete looked back at Jasper. Benny had just come out of the mine and took a coffee cup offered by Jasper. Next they went to a place away from Dave and began to empty the contents of a bucket onto a dirty-looking canvas. There was a lot of equipment set up, and they quickly went to work.

Jasper pounded small rocks into dust with a hammer and placed the remains into glass bottles lined up before him. Then Benny took a butane welding torch out of a case, assembled it, and, with an effort in the failing wind, managed to get it alight. Jasper dusted a strange powder he measured from a tin into bottle caps and put them carefully in front of Benny. He, in turn, gave each one a dainty blast with the flame. They huddled together; Jasper sprinkled the pre-ground rock dust on the heated caps, and Benny once more gave them a quick heat.

Pete tugged Jackstraw close, and whispered. "What are they doing?"

Jackstraw shrugged and stroked his moustache. The fog had come in thickly now, and there was very little visibility. The world was a ghostly grim gray. "It's some sort of test," Jackstraw whispered back frowning, then shook his head. "Not for silver, I'm sure."

"Then what?"

He shrugged again.

"There's that camera or whatever it is again." Pete pointed.

Jackstraw grunted. "It's surely not a camera. But it doesn't matter. The main thing is—how in the wide world are we going to get Dave out of there?"

"He isn't tied."

"But you said there were guns."

Pete nodded miserably.

Whatever test Jasper and Benny had made, it was apparently over, and they both went back inside the mine shaft.

"Can I wave to him?" Pete whispered quickly, but before Jackstraw had time to answer, Jasper and Benny came out of the tunnel, obviously in a great hurry. Pete shrank lower in the scrub, thinking they might have been discovered. Jackstraw ducked low.

At that instant the earth beneath them shook. There was a deep, muffled blast, and the dirt and rocks around them rattled and tumbled over the face of the cliff.

"Dynamite!" gasped Pete.

"But a very small charge," said Jackstraw thoughtfully. "They must be making small test blasts."

Dave hadn't even looked up. The explosions must have been so commonplace he did not pay the slightest heed. Now dust puffed out the shaft, and a swoosh of bats rushed after like smoke from a flue. Benny disappeared into the cave again holding his bucket. Jasper walked to the fire, poured coffee from a blackened pot, and in turn received a sullen sneer from Dave. Then he went back to wait for Benny.

Jackstraw tugged Pete down to the protection of the ridge. He stared at Pete, his eyes bright with excitement.

"You've thought of something!" Pete guessed.

"With your help, we'll have those two trussed up for the spit."

CHAPTER 16

Two Bagged Birds

And that was how, a few minutes later, Pete found himself walking into the reddish earth that was the long-ago diggings of Shadow Mountain Mine. He came into camp behind Dave, yet in clear sight of Jasper. Even so, he was nearly up to the fire and still neither of them had seen him. He stopped. His knees felt like putty, and his hands shook so badly he hardly recognized them as his own.

"Hi—hi, D—Dave," he called weakly.

He might as well have dropped a bomb on them. Jasper dropped his cup with a croak and leaped for the shotgun, which had been half hidden behind some boulders. Dave stumbled to his feet, spilling playing cards every which way, and his mouth dropped open like a stranded fish.

Pete grinned wanly and not very sincerely. He waved halfheartedly, simply to show the stunned Jasper that he hadn't a weapon. Only Crackers, a frantic, wild, uncontainable dog, now she had caught sight of her loving master, was with him.

"Pete!" gasped Dave, completely thunderstruck.

Benny ran out the mine entrance and, with Jasper, circled Pete cautiously.

"I'm here," Pete said a little foolishly, doing his best to play the dunce, letting the dog wind about him tangling herself hopelessly. Dave continued to shake his head in disbelief.

Benny stared at him as if he were a mirage; Jasper gaped openly. Pete walked up to Dave and handed him the struggling Crackers' leash. She was in ecstasy, leaping, panting, licking her tongue over Dave's boots in slavish devotion.

Suddenly Jasper took Pete by the shoulder and gave him a shake that nearly sent him reeling. "How did you get here?" he bellowed.

"Let him alone," Dave threatened.

"It—it's all right, Dave," Pete said shakily.

"Where did you come from?" Benny screeched at him.

"I—I just dug out the cellar and then walked up here."

"Walked?" Jasper screamed at him.

"Well, climbed," corrected Pete. He wiped his tongue over his lips. He could see, in the hazy mists behind all of them, the rope that Jackstraw had dropped down from the ridge above the tunnel. "You see," Pete blurted stupidly, "I couldn't stand being left all alone."

"A mighty far walk," murmured Dave thoughtfully.

"Sure was," Pete replied foolishly. "Farther than I remembered."

"You mean you been here before?" Benny exploded.

Pete nodded nervously.

"He's lying," Jasper hissed.

"No, I'm not. Ask Dave. I came up here about a week ago."

Instantly the two men turned to Dave, and Pete watched his brother face them with as much control as he could summon under the circumstances. Pete swallowed. Dave knew he had never been on top of this silly mountain in his life.

"That's right. He did come up," Dave lied. "A friend of mine does some anthropological work now and then, and he thought it would be a treat to bring Pete to see the burial ground."

"Why didn't you tell us that?" Jasper roared at Pete, and with such vehemence Pete stepped back hastily.

"You"—Pete's voice nearly failed him—"you didn't ask me."

Jasper slammed his hand on his head violently. "Óooo!"

Jackstraw was half down the rope now, a perfect target for Jasper if he should turn suddenly. Pete looked frantically at Dave. His brother had seen Jack-straw, and as he turned to Pete there was a sudden illuminating flash of his eye. "I did come up here!" Pete said frantically, trying to keep the men's attention focused on himself. "Didn't I, Dave?"

"He's right, Jasper. I didn't dare tell you. I was afraid you might have hurt the child more than you did."

Jackstraw was down the line now, half crouched, and ran toward the box holding the dynamite.

"Child!" growled Jasper. "This kid is a teen-age freak."

"I'm only twelve," Pete said heatedly. Jackstraw was back to the rope, and he snaked up it like a monkey. "And I'm not a freak. I just rowed over to the main-land in Dave's old skiff, one you didn't break up, and hiked up to Shadow Mountain. Then I climbed up the trail."

"Yet you shouldn't have come," Dave said very carefully. "Pete, you should have gone straight for the constable."

Pete licked his lips. "But I wanted to be with you," he whined foolishly. Surely even Jasper wouldn't fall for that line. But everything was all right. Jackstraw had the rope up and out of sight.

"He's lying!" Benny rasped flatly. "I know he's lying. I'd better go check the helicopter."

Pete gasped. "Oh! It's all right," he blundered hastily. "It's fine."

The men stopped still and stared at him warily. Pete wondered if he sounded insincere enough. "I just came by," he said a little frantically. "Really, it's quite all right."

"Quick," said Jasper. "Go take a look. We may have to get out fast!"

Pete sat down on the log. His legs didn't seem able to hold him up properly. What if he wasn't doing this right? What if it wasn't what Jackstraw wanted? To top it all, he was nearly ready to burst into tears, and the worst was yet to come.

Dave kneeled beside him and put his hand on his shoulder. "Pete," he said calmly, "I'm real glad you're here." His brother's words gave him the strength he needed, and he sat up straighter.

Then Benny was coming back, running, slipping, awkwardly bumbling through the rocks and brush. He ran straight to Pete and breathlessly yanked him away from Dave. "You little twerp!" he screamed. "What did you do with it?"

Dave was on his feet ready to do battle, but Jasper shoved the shotgun against him, pushing him backward. Pete hung limply from Benny's hand like a rag doll.

"What is it?" Jasper growled.

"The tail rotor's gone," Benny squealed. "This little "What-did-you-do-with-it!"

Dave blinked down at Pete with stunned, startled eyes, which changed slowly to show total admiration.

"Now, now," he soothed carefully. "He's just a little boy."

"Boy!" roared Jasper, and picked Pete up by his collar and shook him until his very teeth rattled. "What-did-you-do-with-it!"

Pete could only hope that Jackstraw had had the time that he needed. With a show of hesitation he finally pointed toward the mine entrance.

"The mine?" gasped Benny, "You put the tail rotor in the mine?"

Pete nodded.

"But that's impossible!"

Pete licked his lips. It most probably was, but he had to try and convince them otherwise. "I—I did," he choked. "It was earlier, when you were over there." He pointed to the place they had made that strange test with the ore from the shaft. He began to tremble, frightened now that perhaps they hadn't been away from the mine entrance for any great length of time. But then to his immense relief a look passed between the men, showing him indecision and uncertainty. When they looked slowly back at him, he knew they were wondering if perhaps he might have done just as he said.

"Go get it!" roared Jasper.

Pete shook his head.

"Get it!" he threatened furiously.

"Don't you hit him, Jasper," Dave growled, and turned to Pete. "It's no use irritating them anymore.

Even if they fly away, they won't be able to get away with this."

Pete shook his head vigorously.

"Pete!" Dave gasped. "Don't be foolish. I don't want you to get hurt. Go get the rotor."

"No," Pete said sharply. "It's dark in there, and I won't go in again. I *won't*." He pushed away from Jasper, stood up, and faced them with a fierceness he didn't at all feel. "You can hit me and shake me and beat me, but I'm not going into that awful black hole again." He stuck out his lip childishly and flung himself into Dave's arms. "Bats are in there, and I almost got blown up!"

Jasper snarled angrily and stomped off to the cave with Benny right behind him.

"I—I put it in the second bend, behind some old timbers," Pete called to them shrilly, only to have Benny glare back unpleasantly, as they disappeared inside the mine.

"Hurry, get down!" Pete gasped to Dave, just as a thunderous blast rocked the cave. A great heave of dirt slid down from above directly over the entrance of the mine, as neatly placed as a door sliding shut. Suddenly Jackstraw was there, the pick hammer in his hand menacingly.

"The guns!" Pete shouted at him. "They have the guns!"

Dave dusted himself off, got to his feet, and ran to meet Jackstraw.

There was a sudden clamoring from inside the mine, and Jasper and Benny began to shout and call out, then began to shove and push the dirt away from the shaft entrance.

"You can stop right there," Jackstraw told them authoritatively. "Try to get out, and I'll blast the rest of the mountain down on top of you." He held out a stick of dynamite in his other hand and motioned Pete and Dave aside. "Throw out your guns!" he shouted to the men.

"Be careful," Pete gasped.

"Throw them out!" commanded Jackstraw, as he crouched behind a huge rock. He put down the pick hammer and struck a match. "You have thirty seconds."

Pete flung himself to the ground. He closed his eyes and covered his ears waiting for the explosion.

"There come the guns!" shouted Dave.

There was a rush of footsteps, a shout, and then Jackstraw gave him a slap on the shoulder. "All over," he said cheerily.

Pete got to his knees and saw Dave running back to them after collecting the firearms. He was smiling broadly.

There were some howls and roars, and Pete peered at the mine entrance, which was now only a tiny slit in size. "Are they all right?" he asked shakily.

"It would seem so," Jackstraw said calmly. "One whale of an argument is going on in there. You did a fine job, Pete."

Dave slapped Jackstraw on the back. "Say, you fixed up the most deserved jail I ever did see." He shook Pete's hand heartily. "You and Pete are the best sights I've ever seen."

Jackstraw grinned and looked around the camp. "Well, now, if you're all that glad to see us, how about filling our empty stomachs? We haven't eaten since sunup."

Dave chuckled happily.

"Can they get out?" Pete asked worriedly. The roars and bawls from the two men had turned into a babble of unpleasant threats.

"Not easily," Jackstraw answered. "It will take a lot of digging, and as far as we're concerned, it's the safest place for them until the constable gets here." He turned to Dave. "Can you tell us what this is all about before we try to get Indian Camp on the helicopter's radio?"

Dave smiled merrily. "Gladly. You really have cooked their goose."

Jackstraw glanced at the work area Jasper and Benny had been using. He kneeled to examine the small blowtorch. "What were they doing? What sort of test is this anyway?"

"Somehow," said Dave, "they got hold of the old mining surveys in Victoria for Shadow Mountain Mine."

"So?" said Jackstraw. "That's no big secret."

Dave nodded. "The mine never had much silver in

it, but the reports had mentioned a good finding of pitchblende along with the silver."

"Pitchblende," said Pete stupidly. "Whatever's that?"

"Silver and pitchblende are often found together," his brother explained. "At the time nobody thought much of it. Now, what with that big find by Great Bear Lake, well—"

"Uranium!" Jackstraw said with a whistle.

Pete felt the hair prickle on his neck and stand out. "But that's even better than diamonds!"

"Diamonds?" questioned Dave helplessly.

Jackstraw grinned. "That was an idea we had on the way up."

"Then that test they were making was for uranium," Pete said eagerly.

Dave nodded. "One of a couple they made. Another was a photographic film test. And they had a Geiger counter."

"The camera!" said Pete. And Jackstraw nodded in understanding.

"What?" said Dave, completely bewildered.

Jackstraw motioned him to continue.

Dave finished filling the coffeepot, put it on to heat, then jabbed his finger toward the mine entrance. "If they found uranium in the mine, they were planning to stake out a claim and register it with the government. They might have made—maybe millions."

"And gone to jail for kidnapping," Pete said sharply.

"Maybe," Dave went on. "It was a risk they took. But by the time someone got me off this knob in the sky where they planned on leaving me, and you, Pete, out of our locked cold cellar, the land would have legally belonged to them. And it would have been our word against theirs." He looked at Jackstraw apologetically. "I don't know if they had any luck with the uranium, but perhaps the engineers will find something this time. I think everyone in the North sort of takes it for granted that even though the lease has expired, all this land up here belongs to the Indians. It's been part of their lives for generations. And now, just think, this might develop into something really tremendous for them."

Jackstraw grunted, and they looked at one another in sincere friendship.

"And if it hadn't been for you two," Dave went on softly, "it might have worked out according to their plan."

Pete looked rather smugly at his brother, but by that time Dave wasn't paying any attention to him. He was trying, uselessly, to keep Crackers from chewing at his boot laces.

"Jackstraw," he said, as he shoved hopelessly at the loving Crackers. "You wouldn't, by any chance, like a good dog at Indian Camp?"

Jackstraw laughed. "I should certainly say not!" But unexpectedly he put his hand on Pete's shoulder. "But how about Pete here," he said seriously. "He would make a pretty fine Indian, and I'd take him any day."

Pete sucked in his breath sharply. No greater compliment could any man ever give him.

"That is," went on Jackstraw with a twinkle in his eye, "if he can just find that tail rotor still buried back there someplace, so we can give it to the constable."